THE WOLF'S LAIR

The Wolf's Lair

J. K. Little

Published in 2019 by

J. K. Little

ISBN (paperback) 978-1-9163154-0-2

ISBN (ebook) 978-1-9163154-1-9

Cover Design and Interior Layout by designforwriters.com

Prologue
First Meeting

"*Nein, Nein, Nein*" was the repeating blast I was becoming all too familiar with. "*Sie sind ein lungner und ein feind vom Vaterland*": I was a liar, and an enemy of the Fatherland. I gulped as the translator spoke the words I had been expecting for the past hour. "I will have you taken out and shot, if one more word comes out of your treacherous mouth."

The cold, damp musty scent in the badly lit room I stood in had long since bothered me. I wondered whether I had made a huge mistake. Standing here right now was an opportunity way beyond anything I had ever dreamt possible in my wildest fantasies.

I had always been fascinated by the histories of World War Two. As a kid growing up, I watched scores of old World War Two movies and then re-enacted them with my ever-growing collection of toy soldiers. I would play out the manoeuvres and the battles and determine how I would have done things differently. I remember as a schoolboy hating most school studies but when I got my first secondary school history book, and saw those old black-and-white pictures of the battlefields and masses of panzer divisions squaring off against the mighty T34 tanks of the Russian Red Army, my imagination would switch into overdrive as I worked out who would come out on top; the stories of how and why decisive battles were won and lost.

I pondered the disastrous decisions of those Panzer Division commanders trying to use blitzkrieg manoeuvres through the heavy forest areas of the Ardennes, with fuel scarce for tanks during the battle of the Bulge. The Blitzkrieg relied on fast-moving armoured divisions, backed up by the fierce-fighting and battle-hardened, loyal but ruthless Waffen SS, with air support from the German Luftwaffe. Or maybe the German tank commanders already knew it was a mistake, but their objections fell on deaf ears? Hitler gambled and lost. At that stage of the war Germany was hanging on by a thread. "The Battle of the Bulge", as one newspaper named it, was the last great hope of Hitler to halt the advancing American and British armed forces. The last chance for the Third Reich to hold the Allies back, split the English and American troops, and then hope for a peace pact to give the German army time to rebuild, rearm and turn their attention to the East and Russia. But the cold, harsh conditions of the Ardennes, the narrow, muddy roads and hillsides, slowed the counter-offensive of the German army. Small pockets of success were achieved by some German commanders but throughout the offensive named "Unternehmen Wacht am Rhein"—translated as "Watch on the Rhine"—the main battle was lost, doomed from the start, forcing the Germans back into a defensive position and back deep into Germany. Back home towards Berlin.

Now, 29th June 1941, six days after Hitler arrived, here I was, incredible as it may sound, standing in the Wolfsschanze; or, as we in the English-speaking world know it, the Wolf's Lair – the Headquarters for Operation Barbarossa, the German invasion of the Soviet Union. I had to use my words to fight for my life, and for my goal.

"I am not lying, and if you do not listen to what I have to say you will be remembered in history as the most hated, vile and evil leader that ever existed. This, I can assure you," I shouted back. The German translator was sweating somewhat, standing still with awkward hands and waiting for us to speak in turn. "You will lose this war, and you will lose it disastrously. I can help you win and change your destiny. The way it should have been." I could hardly believe the words coming from my own mouth.

Rounding his large paper-filled wooden desk, he approached and stood two feet away from me, and turned his head up to meet mine. His cold eyes buried deep into mine and he held my gaze for what felt like an eternity. Two SS Guards stood close by in eager readiness to strike if I moved a muscle in his direction.

Yes: Adolf Hitler was standing in front of me and piercing me with his overpowering glare.

I struggled to stay calm, but held firm. Finally, he turned and ordered his guards out. They hesitated. "*Steigen Sie aus, steigen Sie aus.*" The guards looked at each other then gave me one last warning stare. Turning back towards their leader, they clicked their heels obediently and roared, "*Heil* Hitler," then quickly exited the room, closing the heavy steel bunker door behind them.

His interpreter stayed to translate. He was a small stout man with fat fingers and chubby cheeks. He stood awkwardly when spoken to as if fearing making a mistake. His uniform didn't fit him well and I doubted the medals on his SS shirt were ever earned in battle. But apart from this puppet, there I was alone in a bunker with arguably the most hated man in history, trying to persuade this dictator of what had cost him the war; the mistakes he had made. The stupid, vanity-driven decisions that had destroyed his dreams for a greater, supreme Germany, his thousand-year Reich.

But why, you want to know? Why, and how? Why would anyone but a Nazi-loving, Hitler fanatic, Jew-hating redneck want to help Adolf Hitler? The man who oversaw the extermination of six million Jews; the man who brought war and destruction to Europe, resulting in the deaths of tens of millions of soldiers and civilians.

More incredibly: how was I able to stand there in East Prussia, June 1941, with the Führer of Germany, when I was born on

January 29th 1978, in Dublin, Ireland? I was a twenty-five-year-old Irish man from a normal working-class family, and yet here I was.

Hitler kept looking at me, nodding quickly up and down. My body started to shake uncontrollably. And as I gulped, and glanced quickly over at the interpreter, I saw he was open-mouthed as he too waited for the next words to come out of Hitler's mouth. Without speaking a word, the man in front of me raised his hand and waited for me to grasp it. In near-disbelief I looked at his pale hand and gave him my shaking hand in return. With three shakes he let it go.

He smiled at me, said nothing, turned and walked slowly back behind his desk. He looked down at a large map laid out, pushing aside some papers. As I watched him study his maps, I saw he held that smile for some time.

And that was the start of an extraordinary journey I had instigated; a change that could bring terrifying consequences and everlasting ruin to our world if my true plans were discovered.

Perhaps I had better go back to the very beginning.

Chapter 1
Doctor Hoitdle

"HEY, JOHN, WAIT UP," CALLED a scruffily-dressed man running to catch me up as I left the college building. It was the last day of college, 27th May 2003, and I had just handed in my final history paper to Professor Hartley, to whom I had been senior assistant for the past three years; now I was heading home.

"What are you doing later?" my rather loud friend Paul Duffy shouted. He was a real college-head: scruffy clothes, rough hairdo, and shirt hanging out; you know the type. Not that he didn't have money – or at least his family did. But he felt he had to look the part, I guess. He was twenty-four and studying arts and drama which was right up his street. We first met on my second day of college, I was eighteen years old and he a few months younger; I found myself wandering around the corridors looking for my next class on modern history. Somehow, I found myself in a bathroom where I came across Paul smoking weed out of the partially-opened window. He was so laid-back about it, looked at me and offered me a puff which I politely declined. But he was able to at least tell me which classroom 4C was. Anyway, as I was leaving the bathroom, I clocked one of the lecturers heading towards us, so I darted back in and warned him of the oncoming danger, and he chucked the smoke out of the window and ran into a cubicle. I left him there and carried on with my day, until after college that evening. I was heading for my bus stop, when guess who comes up behind me and almost jumps on my back with a big, "Yo, thanks man, you saved my ass!" After that we started hanging out and, well, he kind of grew on me. We've been friends ever since.

"Nothing much," I said. "There's a documentary on at nine tonight about the generals of World War Two."

"Man, can't you ever think of anything else besides Hitler and World War-fucking-Two, dude? I mean, come on, we got the whole summer to plan. You know, drinking, girls, getting high, drinking and girls," he said.

"You said drinking and girls twice," I replied.

"Yeah, man, that's because I plan on doing them on the double each time, know what I mean?" he said shiftily, raising his eyebrows up and down like Groucho Marx.

"Only too well!" I said.

"Hey, come out with us tonight. We're all meeting up in the city tonight at about eight thirty, okay? You can record that shit and get out and live a little. I have a few friends for us to meet up with. You know, a few friends with benefits," he said with another grin.

"Okay – who are we talking about now?" I asked.

"Em… Okay, you remember hot Jenny with the fine ass from my English class? Well, her and her room-mate Carly who happens to be a trainee nurse," he gloated. "You don't have to thank me," he continued, smirking. "Do it for me, I need my wing man." I knew he would pester me all day until I gave in, so I agreed.

I started to enter a reminder in my phone when Paul asked, "What are you doing?"

"I'm setting a reminder to record that documentary tonight," I replied.

"Shit, man, you really need to chill out," he bellowed, and off he went.

"See you later," I shouted after him. He just put one hand in the air and gave a triumphant fist.

On the way home, I stopped in my local grocer shop to pick up the day's newspapers and a packet of gum. The bus-stop was just two minutes' walk from Trinity College. From there the bus ride was only ten minutes out of the city into Fairview, where I got off at the Malahide road and Fairview junction. Then a short walk to my rented apartment. While waiting to cross the road at Fairview I took out a stick of gum, undid the wrapper and placed the gum into my mouth. I waited for a clear gap in the stream of traffic and made a dash for it. I got to the other side and stopped to adjust my backpack; I noticed a tall old man, standing against a wall I passed daily, just watching me. As I looked more closely, he turned away to avoid my stare. I thought nothing of it and kept walking but even approaching the gate to my apartment entrance, I still had a sense I was being watched. I turned around suddenly. The man had stepped out from the wall and was just staring at me. It was unnerving.

I shouted towards him, "Are you ok? Can I help you with something?" He was wearing a long, light brown trench coat and a brown hat. He must have been about six feet tall, wore small spectacles and appeared to hunch over slightly. He had a worn leather briefcase in his right hand. His shoes were heavy and black, and his trousers were grey pinstriped. He stood and stared at me for a few moments and then turned and walked away out of view.

Weirdo, I thought to myself. Opening the gate, I went through and closed it behind me before climbing the steps to my door. Taking one last look back, I could not see the man. Locking the door behind me, I walked into the living room and threw my backpack on the worn armchair then went into the kitchen and clicked on the kettle.

I turned on the TV to catch the six o'clock news but just as the programme was about to start, I heard a noise at the front door. I came out into the hall and noticed a brown envelope lying on the floor. As I picked it up, I peered through the spyhole in the front door but could see nothing. I unlocked the door and opened it with one foot close to the bottom, so it could not be pushed in on me if someone was waiting on the other side. I glanced sideways around the door.

"Anyone there?" I asked. When no reply came, I opened the door fully and stepped outside. I could not see anyone expect for a middle-aged mother dragging her shopping and her two offspring behind her. I took one last look around to make sure I could see no one; I was particularly looking for the tall man in the trench coat who had made me feel uneasy earlier.

I looked down at the envelope and observed it had my name written in full: John Joseph Ryan. I had never received a letter from anyone with my middle name; in fact, I don't remember ever really using it. I turned and went back inside, this time using the chain as well as locking the door.

I walked back into the kitchen and placed the envelope on the table. I put a teabag in my Manchester United mug and poured in the boiled water and stirred the teabag all the while still looking back at the envelope. I took a carton of milk out of the fridge and poured in the last few drops.

"Need more milk," I thought. Sipping the tea, I decided to open the envelope.

I pulled a chair out from my small kitchen table and sat down. I started to slowly rip open the envelope from the top and across. I looked inside and noticed it had an old black-and-white photo, paper-clipped to a letter folded in two. I pulled them both out and unclipped the photo and looked at it first. It was a picture of a man smiling and shaking hands with Adolf Hitler with various other men in SS uniforms standing nearby. I had never seen this picture before, in any of my research, and I had done as much research work on Adolf Hitler and the Third Reich as most historians in their field.

I picked up the letter, which had only six lines in perfect hand-written script.

I very much enjoyed your work and your prognosis of

the Two Sides. It was not only enlightening, insightful and brilliantly written, but it also had a sense of imagination, honesty and fairness never published before and you showed an incredible amount of bravery to write what others have failed to see.

We will meet soon.
R.H.

"Who the hell is R.H.?" I thought. And why was he impressed by my *Two Sides* work?

Two Sides was a look at what would have happened had Hitler won the war. Yes, other historians and writers have asked those same questions many times over, but I wanted to look at other facts and ideas I felt were overlooked in history books written over the past century, which I argued needed to be brought to the fore.

While writing *Two Sides*, I had had to make certain that I was no way fighting Hitler's corner or making excuses for what the Nazis did before and during World War Two. But I was compelled by a quote I once read: "The victors get to write the history books." And so, I wrote the following theory paper:

Most of the world now knows that the Jewish people were persecuted by the Nazis during the 1930's and 1940's, but would we have known about those atrocities if Germany had won the war? Probably not, or at least we could have a very toned-down version of those horrific events. But that's just my point. For example, do the history books portray Joseph Stalin in that same light? No. And why not? Because Stalin and his Red Army were victorious! Over the passage of time we forget that many so-called 'civilized countries' terror-ised other nations too weak to defend themselves. The British Empire for one, ruled by the Kings and Queens of England. At its peak, the British Empire was the largest empire in the world. Do you think that happened by diplomatic means? How many people lost their lives in that global expansion? How many countries were ruled and held under colonization by this so-called civilized nation? It is too long a list to mention, but in its time Britain has, at some point in history, invaded and established a military presence in one hundred and seventy-one places including Singapore, India, Canada and, of course, our very own homeland, Ireland, which has been divided into North and South and been the cause of many more deaths.

How many of these people were slaves? What we would think today if Britain had black slaves running their homes, businesses and working in their fields? These poor people were dragged away from their families, screaming in terror. The children running to help their mothers and fathers were kicked out of the way by these slave traders. There, the traders would force them into heavy chains and march them off to waiting ships. They would be thrown into the bellies of these ships and locked in dark, filthy galleys, fearing where they were going and what would happen to them. Sound familiar to anyone?

I give you *The Great British Empire*.

Those slaves would have seen the St George's Cross flag flapping about in the wind as they were beaten on board.

Replace that George's Cross flag with a swastika, and would you notice the difference? But although we don't look back at that period and think of the British Empire as evil, black-hating dictators, we do with Adolf Hitler. And rightly so! However, I cannot understand why he's the only one. Well, in fact I can understand:

because the British were the victors and ruled many lands!

Why is Alexander the III of Macedonia not villainised? Or, as he is better known, Alexander the Great!

His place in history is one secured by his incredible bravery, foresight and pure drive to rule the known world. He was a man with incredible military tactical ability. But how many people died because of his crusade? Not only his "enemies", but his own people too. Alexander the Great: what was so "Great" about this conqueror? Did Hitler not want to rule the world too? Is it because we think, 'well, that was 300 B.C. and it's not that important to us except in history books'? We see his crusade as legendary, great battles and conquests to be taught and treasured. Don't generals of today measure themselves against this great Macedonian King?

People could argue that he fought against armies and did not murder innocent people – well, my argument is that he did. Hundreds of thousands of soldiers were forced to fight for one man's dream. I ask you, does this sound familiar? More died in World War Two because of advances in technology: tanks, the Air Force, bombs, machine guns and, of course, eventually the atomic bomb. People lived in large, crowded cities, so of course more died. Do you think Alexander the Great would not have used a bomb on a city, given the chance, to win?

Of course, he would. Would Napoleon? I believe so.

But these people are studied and admired as either mythical heroes, in the case of Alexander the Great, or as tragic, in the case of Napoleon, who in fact fought more battles than Alexander the Great, Hannibal, Julius Caesar, Gustavas Adolphus and Frederick the Great combined.

Did these military leaders have any real respect for human lives? I think we like to think they did in some way, and that their destiny was to be great military commanders; to believe that it was something in their blood, written in the stars. But then why not Hitler?

My point is this: they were all blood-crazed dictators who had a thirst for destruction, brutality and totalitarian rule. They wanted history to remember them as great leaders of their time and to be acknowledged for their tactical superiority. But how many people died and suffered because of their egos? We know many did, but in their case we gloss over it as secondary to the interesting facts we really want to learn about, like the great battles they fought and how they tried to outwit each other on the battlefield. We look at old films portraying the Roman Empire marching in numerous rectangular block formations and wait with bated breath as they drew closer to their enemy. Waiting for the clash, we smelled blood. We wanted blood. But they were people. They had sons and daughters and wives back at home. It is glossed over.

We wanted the blood.

What makes a million Jewish deaths different from a million Russian deaths? How about thirty million Russian deaths? What am I talking about?

Hitler had ordered the death of the Jewish people – the 'Final Solution', as the Nazis called it. He wanted to exterminate their race. He failed; however, the Nazis did succeed in murdering over six million Jews during World War Two.

But how many people know that Joseph Stalin had over thirty million of his own people killed through starvation with his five-year plan to build Russia into an industrial and economic power? The upheaval in the agricultural sector disrupted food production, resulting in widespread famine, and was known in the Ukraine as the *Holodomor*, 'Death by Starvation'. He had his so-called Enemies of the State either executed or sent to the Gulag labour camps, where they rarely survived.

Even after the war, when the Soviet Union took control of many eastern European countries behind what became known as the Iron Curtain, many more died under his rule. But Stalin was a victor; Russia was one of the main reasons why Germany lost the war. Just as for Napoleon, Russia proved a bridge too far for Germany, and they had to retreat. We now know that the invasion by Germany on Russia was a mistake. So, Stalin took the plaudits, as did his allies after the War, and forced his people under harsher communist conditions than ever before leading to further fear and death.

Of course, Stalin eventually died in March 1953. When his successor Nikita Khrushchev took over, he denounced Stalin's legacy and drove the process of de-Stalinization of the Soviet Union. Stalin was a tyrant just like Hitler. But Stalin had won.

We know today the Iron Curtain across many countries under Russia's control fell, most notably the Berlin Wall.

Over the years, one by one countries like Bulgaria, Poland, Hungary, Czechoslovakia, Romania, Albania and East Germany broke loose from Soviet rule. The world become smaller, and Russia could no longer hold its grip on these people. Over history we have seen so many times great empires ruling weaker nations, but they all fall eventually.

The Roman and British Empires; the Macadonian-ruled kingdom of Alexander the Great. The people rebelled and got their freedom, even closer to home as in Scotland and in the Republic of Ireland.

And this, I believe, is what would have happened if Germany had won the war under Hitler.

I have held many deep discussions, with anyone willing to listen, arguing that this is exactly how I would have envisaged this alternative view of history.

We would not know about the Holocaust. We would have heard rumors, of course, stories from people who were there. But there would be no film evidence, no black-and-white photographs like the ones we see in today's history books.

And it's just as well we can see this today, to teach us all a lesson about cruelty. We must see this, we must learn, we must know what happened to Jewish people and to others in these death camps. However, we must know about all the injustices of the world, not just those of the Jewish people. What happened to those poor souls was an atrocity, but they do not have a monopoly on suffering. To be clear, I do not assume that the Jewish community demand a monopoly on suffering. But it can be depicted that way in our history books, documentaries and movies today.

All I want is equality across all injustices, and to show people that there were many equally evil tyrants as Hitler over the course of history, and it must not be that because they won their wars, their actions are glossed over and they get to portray their side of events in whichever way they see fit.

To illustrate this, here is a hypothetical event. It's 1942, and Hitler has achieved victory over the Russians. Troops are regrouped and sent back to the west to concentrate their military power against the assumed eventual invasion into Europe by American and British-led Allied forces. They bunker down, dig in and fortify the coastlines even further. Both sides come to the realization that they could be in a stalemate. But Hitler has achieved his main objectives. He has gained stability, vast wealth, and industrial power from ruling Russia. So, after years of fighting Hitler, Churchill and Roosevelt decide on a ceasefire. Germany consolidate and control most of Europe, Scandinavia, Eastern Europe, Russia and all its states, the Ukraine and Belarus. France is left alone, and over the course of the next three years the Allies phase out their army and return home. Now Germany under Adolf Hitler is running its controlled countries, just as Stalin did with puppet leaders after World War Two.

Neither Western countries nor Russia ever get into Poland or other Nazi-controlled countries, so we never get to find out the truth about the death camps and the other atrocities committed.

Roll on another few years, and schoolchildren are learning about the great battles fought by both sides. They discuss the incredible blitzkrieg manoeuvers of the German army and how they would use lighting strikes against the enemy and then surround them in a pincer manoeuver.

Hitler would have his legacy. German history books would see him as a great leader. They would experience economic boom from increased the agriculture and economic wealth they amassed from oil-rich countries like the Ukraine and Russia. The iron and steel industries would be in full flow. Hitler would be the German saviour: 'Our Führer.' His picture would adorn every household in all of Germany and across German-controlled territories. Statues of him would be everywhere. The German people would feel no shame about the war.

Then in 1956 Hitler's health deteriorates and he dies after suffering a stroke. There is a week of national mourning. Leaders from across the world offer their condolences, whether they mean them or not. They must be seen to be graceful and diplomatic.

A new leader takes control: probably a high-ranking Nazi, maybe Himmler or Goebbels.

Many more years pass, and we are into the 1970s. The people in the German-controlled states are becoming increasingly restless with their German oppressors and demand their freedom. Other countries like England and the USA ask for democracy. Many people die in protests across the Baltic States, Romania and Hungary.

Ten years later, Hungary eventually gets its freedom and so starts the fall of the German Third Reich. The German people have long moved on since Hitler and Himmler are now dead. A reformist takes over and starts the process, looking at opening borders for better trade and economic growth in times of the global market to avoid getting left behind.

It's now 1987, and the final German-controlled state of Russia is freed and given its democracy. The world rejoices and hails Germany as a modern power with new goodwill and openness. Their leader is given the Nobel Peace Prize and meets the US President in the White House.

However, calls from the Jewish community still trying to get files opened on relatives who went missing during World War Two continue to fall on deaf ears. The German leadership deny any involvement in so-called 'Jewish Death Camps' and ask for the Jewish community to move on and to accept that all countries lost lives, and it's time to heal old wounds and let sleeping dogs lie.

Indeed, it's a fictional depiction of what I think could have happened. But I firmly believe that it is a plausible account of how what could have played out, based on the rise and fall of the Soviet Union during its Iron Curtain grip on Eastern Europe.

One man can and try to rule the world, but it always comes crumbling down in the end. Nothing lasts forever. There is always someone else with another idea, another ideal on how the world should be. It takes an enormous amount of passion and drive to do what many of the aforementioned leaders have done and tried to do but we must not forget that it does not mean we can excuse any of these on the mere basis that they won their war. There are two sides to every story…but the victors got to write the history books.

When I submitted this paper to Professor Hartley, I was a little wary of how it could be perceived. But I had studied under Professor Hartley for three years at that point and knew if anyone understood what I was trying to say, it would be him. And so it proved. I earned not only an A plus for the year, but a position as a junior research assistant for the next three years whilst I obtained my Master's if I so desired. And desired it, I did. Professor Hartley loved to be challenged and I believe it I was able to tap into that. He lost his twenty two year old only son David some years earlier in a hiking accident and took six months off work to deal with the tragedy. I think he liked me being around and always made time for me when I needed help with a project or pointing me in the right direction for exams. It had almost become a kind of father-son relationship. There were times when he accidently called me David and when he did, he would always apologise, but I would never comment. I suppose I felt sorry for him and it was nice to have a kind of father figure in my life. Someone that I could look up to and ask for advice. While the relationship was mainly an academic one, it felt much more than that.

I put the letter and photo back into the envelope and placed it on the kitchen table.

I still had that eerie feeling of being watched. I walked to the kitchen window and looked outside into the small, unkept garden and looked around. Not seeing anything suspicious I lowered the blinds fully. I turned and walked out of the kitchen and decided to close all the curtains in the apartment and check all the windows and door locks just to be sure. At each window, I took a quick glance around to make sure nobody was out there watching me.

Once I had completed my security checks, I went back into the kitchen to see what I was going to eat for dinner. I took out the one remaining frozen pizza from the freezer and turned on the oven to pre-heat. With time to spare I decided to have a shower. I left the kitchen and into the ensuite bedroom just next door, stripped off and got into the shower. While showering quicker than normal and pricking my ears for any noises outside, I had uneasy thoughts of the creepy old man lurking about. Once I was dried off, I dressed in casual clothing, faded blue jeans, white t-shirt, worn black socks and brown leather loafers. Casual but smart, I thought. I picked up my bottle of Hugo Boss aftershave and sprayed it onto my neck and hands, rubbing it on my face and around my wrists.

Oven should be ready, I thought. Before heading back into the kitchen, I picked up my mobile phone off the bed locker and noticed a text from Paul. *'Yo, heil John, don't forget tonight. We're meeting in Murphy's at 8:30pm. Paul.'* I replied with a simple thumbs up emoji then threw the phone onto the bed.

I continued into the kitchen and pulled the frozen pizza out of its box and wrapping and placed it carefully onto a tray and into the oven. *Another twenty minutes to kill*, I thought. I sat down at the table, flicking through the TV channels looking for anything worth watching and stopped at a wildlife documentary about sharks.

A while later, after finishing my pizza and cleaning up, I decided to make tracks. I turned off the TV and retrieved my mobile phone and keys. Checking my watch, I saw it was 8:19. I left the kitchen and hallway lights on and heading for the door, I grabbed my coat off the hall rack and put it on. I unlocked the door and took a long look around. It was dark out, but the many streetlamps outside gave me good visibility of the surrounding area. I did not notice anyone in particular and closed the door behind me. I walked down the steps and out through the gate, closing it after me. I felt a bit more relaxed now and started thinking of our double date tonight; I hoped Paul hadn't set me up with a bore, or an ugly duckling.

I headed up Fairview strand., crossing over the wide road again to head for the bus stop. It wouldn't take me long to ride the bus into the city centre, and only five minutes from leaving the bus to Murphy's. I was running a little late, but Paul wouldn't mind, as he'd be too busy chatting up every girl in a ten-foot radius.

As I neared the bus stop, I got a shiver down my spine. I turned around and standing behind me was the old man that I saw staring at me only hours earlier. "What do you want?" I said, trying to sound stern. "Are you following me?"

"Forgive me if I've unnerved you, Mr. Ryan," the man replied, with a soft foreign accent. "I need to speak with you about an urgent matter, if I could have just a few moments of your time?"

"Speak to me about what? Who are you?" I said.

"Oh, how rude of me! My name is Doctor Ralf Hoitdle, and I need to speak to you in relation to your – how shall I say? Your insight into German history, if I may?"

"What do you want to know about it, and how do you know me?"

"Oh, Mr. Ryan, we have known about you for some time now," he said knowingly.

It was the *we know you* part that spooked me. "Look, I don't know you, or who 'we' are, but I'm getting this next bus to meet some friends. A lot of friends," I added, "so if you need to speak to me, maybe we could meet up tomorrow in the daytime?" He stepped forward to get closer to me and I moved back a step.

"Did you recognize the man in the photo?" he asked.

"The man with Hitler, I assume you are referring to?" I enquired.

"Yes."

"No, I don't know who he is. Why, should I?"

"That man, my dear Mr. Ryan, is your grandfather," he said knowingly. I just stood there open mouthed. "Yes, I can see how that would shock you a little," he continued.

"Shock me? I think you've got the wrong person," I replied. "My grandfather died before the war in England, while working as a lab technician. He was never in Germany, or continental Europe for that matter. He died while driving home one rainy night and lost control of his car and crashed into a ditch and was killed instantly. He would never have met Hitler."

"Ah yes, that's what your father probably told you. And I was very sorry to hear of his passing, too, by the way," he said.

"How do you know of my father? You know what, this is all a little too weird, so I'm going to ask you to leave, please," I insisted.

Just then the bus came around the bend and slowed to pull up at the bus stop. I started to get on when he shouted to me, "I sense you want to know more, Mr. Ryan." Pointing over the road, Hoitdle said, "I'll be at O'Connor's café across the road at eleven in the morning. I hope to see you there. If not, no hard feelings. Oh, and enjoy your night. Carly seems like a wonderful girl." How the hell did he know anything about a girl I was yet to meet? I was about to shout that out, when the door of the bus closed. I paid my fare and went to the back of the bus and sat down staring out of the back window; I watched him as the bus pulled away. Neither of us took our eyes off each other until the bus pulled around a bend and he was out of sight. I took in a sigh of relief and relaxed into my seat.

Jesus, I thought. *Could he be telling the truth? Why would my father lie to me about my Grandad? Was there some kind of secret in the family?* It had never seemed strange that my parents had no photographs of my Grandad, Joseph Ryan. *Forget about it*, I thought. *It's not true. Someone is trying to spook me over my 'Two Sides' paper.* Someone from the Jewish community probably pissed off at me, I guessed, and not for the first time too; many letters of complaints had arrived at the university after my paper was published in the local newsletter and ended up going viral.

The bus pulled into its last stop, and everyone got off the bus. I walked fast, and ended up getting to the pub at eight forty-five. Inside, Murphy's was a little more crowded than usual. It was a small pub with a few nooks and crannies, so if you could manage to get an empty space, you could relax and enjoy a conversation without everyone bumping off you as they passed to get to the bar or toilet. It had a mixture of local city centre and banking sector about it, yet the clientele seemed to mix quite well. Just when I thought I'd be standing all night, with a pint in my hand, I spotted Paul at the bar with two girls I assumed were our dates for the night. He had managed to grab and keep hold of four stools at the far corner of the pub, where the crowd wouldn't be pushing past us. He spotted me and raised his arm up, yelling out, "Over here, geek!" I nodded back, and headed over.

"Hey you made it, what are you having?"

"The usual," I replied.

"Yo, Tony, one Guinness, and a Coors Light for the fag here,"

"Alright, alright," I replied. I liked Coors Light. It didn't make me burp up all night which I found a lot of other beers did.

"Hi, you must be John," the pretty blonde girl sitting next to Paul said. I recognized her from being around the college; she was indeed in Paul's English class. She was medium height, at about five foot six. She had fake tan on her legs and arms, but not overdone and she was wearing a short white skirt, black strappy heels and a pink tight-fitting top that showed off her very womanly curves. Her hair was medium-length to the shoulder, wavy, and her make-up wasn't too heavily applied. She wore a white silk scarf tied around her neck, around her neck, and it was refreshing to see she wasn't caked in and stinking of fake tan. She smelled great, too, with a gentle perfume flowing up into my nostrils.

She was indeed an attractive girl.

"Yeah, hi," I replied.

"Oh, shit man, sorry, I should have introduced you. This is Carly, Jenny's roommate. The nurse," Paul added in a *you know what I mean* voice.

"Hi John, nice to meet you," Carly said, holding out her hand.

"Hi, nice to meet you too," I replied, shaking her hand.

"And this is Jenny – my secret crush, but not so secret anymore," Paul chuckled in Jenny's direction.

"Oh, shut up, Paul," Jenny retorted, and gave him a friendly slap on the shoulder. Jenny had dark hair tied up in a ponytail, and she wore white jeans, and a black satin top. She was not as attractive as Carly, I thought to myself, but still very pretty. She was carrying a few more pounds than Carly, but she carried it well. Her knee-high black boots gave her an air of authority and she probably needed it to keep Paul in his place.

The drinks arrived, and Paul handed me my pint. "Man, I needed that," I said, taking a gulp.

"Why's that?" Paul questioned.

"Had some creep hanging around the apartment today when I got home, and he was still there when I went to get the bus into the city. Came over and said he knew my Grandad during the war."

"And why is this weird?" Paul asked. But I didn't really want to get into all this again with the girls here, so I just said, "Ah, don't worry about it. I'll talk to you tomorrow about it, if that's okay?" Paul just nodded and said, "Sure."

"So, you're a nurse, Carly?" I asked.

"Yes, that's right," she replied. "I'm at work placement in the Accident and Emergency room in the Mater Hospital."

"Wow, that must keep you busy all day and night," I replied.

"It can be tough alright, but I love the job and the people I work with too," she said.

The night was turning out okay, and I was getting on well with Carly. I had forgotten all about the day's events and was totally engrossed in our four-way conversation. Paul was in full swing with the jokes and I felt a good vibe from my newfound nightingale.

"Last orders, ladies and gents," Tony yelled out to start the wind-down.

Knocking back the last of our drinks, Jenny asked, "What about a night cap back at our place?"

Just as I was about to call it a night, Paul didn't hesitate to yell out, "Yeah, great, we are so there!" Carly looked at me and said, "Is that ok with you, John?"

"Yeah, sure, no problem, love to," I replied like a stuttering dork.

"Great, let's go," Jenny jumped in. "Our apartment is just five minutes' walk from here." We got up, put our jackets and coats on, and left the pub.

Turning left down Westmorland Street, we laughed and joked along the way. Most of the pubs were emptying out the drunken revellers as people were either trying to hail taxis, queue up for fast food or head for the late-night disco bars.

The girls walked on a little bit as Paul dropped back with me and put his arm around my shoulder and said, "Well, bro, I think our luck is in tonight."

"Relax," I replied. "We're only heading back for a nightcap, so don't get too cocky."

"Yeah, yeah, I know what I'm going back for," he said, with that knowing grin on his face.

We rounded the next corner off Porter Street and walked about two hundred yards before stopping at a large red door with a brass letterbox and doorknob. "We're here," the girls said.

Jenny took out her keys and opened the door. We followed the girls into the sitting room where they told us to relax. Carly opened a cabinet door to reveal a row of alcohol: a half-empty sherry bottle, Bacardi, whiskey, and an unopened bottle of red wine, which looked like a Merlot.

"Help yourselves, boys, we'll be back in a minute," Jenny said.

Paul took out the Bacardi and looked for some glasses. He found them in the press above and took out four glasses and started to pour.

Shouting from the upstairs bedroom, Carly said, "There are mixers in the fridge in the kitchen if you're looking for them."

I went out to get them and headed for the kitchen. The lights were already on. I opened the fridge door and found a bottle of Coke. I walked back to the living room and handed it to Paul.

He opened the bottle, poured the coke into all four glasses and handed me one and took one for himself. We both just looked at photos and paintings placed on the walls and nodded to each other in an *I'll guess we'll just wait and see* look.

I sat down on the two-seater sofa and Paul eventually sat down in one of the two worn chairs in the corner of the small sitting room.

"Hey Paul, could you come up here a minute?" Jenny called out from upstairs.

Paul got up and yelled out, "Yeah, on my way." He looked at me as he headed out the door and said, "Have fun my friend, see ya in the morning." I hadn't even time to reply before he was gone.

With my head tilted towards the door, I heard him heading up the wooden stairs; then I heard a door close behind him, and Jenny's giggle made me realize that this girl was a fast mover and Paul was in for a fun night.

I sipped my Bacardi and Coke and sank back into the sofa. I didn't hear Carly walk in until she said, "Hey, you ok?" I jumped and sat up straight in my seat; I tried to look coy but was glad to see her. She nodded towards my glass. "Can I have one of those?"

"Yeah, sure," I replied. Before I could get up and head for the pre-poured drinks in the drinks cabinet that Paul had made earlier, Carly came towards me and said, "Wait, let me try yours."

"Okay… are you sure you don't want a fresh one?"

"This will be fine," she said in a soft voice.

I reached out to hand her the glass but instead of taking it off me she put her hands around mine and pulled them in with the glass and eased it to her lips. She tipped it back and knocked it back in one. Licking her lips, she smiled and said, "That went down well, how was it for you?" I blushed. "Come on," she said, and led me by one hand out the door and up the stairs. As we reached the top, I could hear Paul and Jenny still giggling in the room next to the bathroom. Without paying attention Carly headed to the next bedroom on the left of the hallway and brought me inside. I noticed she had prepared some soft music in the background and scented candles burning on her dresser and the bedside lamp was covered with a red scarf.

She sat on the bed and patted it beside her to beckon me over. I obeyed without hesitation and gazed into her eyes for a few moments. I felt my heart beating that bit faster. I could see her eyes trace to my lips and back to my eyes again and then she leaned in and gently pressed her lips against mine and kissed me softly. I felt myself getting instantly aroused. Carly had such soft lips and she was a very sensual kisser.

As we slowly started to strip each other I realized that Paul wasn't the only one in for a great night.

Carly stood up and was standing in front of me in just her white bra and panties and I scanned my eyes over her amazing toned body. She turned around away from me and swayed side to side to the music. Then walking backwards, she backed right into me, so I could rub my hand up her tight body. She sat down into my lap and I helped her out of her bra and dropped it to the floor. I slid my hands around her sides and onto her breasts and felt the hardness of her nipples. She turned her head and we kissed for a long time before easing ourselves under the covers for what was a night to remember. Carly was – well, let's just say she was one fine, adventurous lady, and I had a night that I would remember for a long time.

Waking up to sounds of birds chirping and cars driving by mixed with voices coming from downstairs, I noticed I was alone in the bed; I looked out the small window, happy it was Saturday and I had nothing to do. I lay back and smiled after remembering the night's erotic adventures.

I sat up and reached for my watch to see it was 10:13 a.m.

Just then the door opened, and Carly walked in wearing a silky dressing gown with the ties hanging loose. Underneath, I glimpsed a silky pink thigh-high nightie; she looked amazing.

"Good morning. Thought you might be hungry after your exploits last night," she said with a cheeky grin. "I made toast, croissants and coffee for my lover."

"Thank you! You look great by the way," I told her.

"Why thank you, Sir," she said in a funny American accent. Laying the tray on the bed she went around to my side and pushed in beside me. "Are you in a hurry today? do you need to be anywhere?"

"No, I don't think so," I replied hesitantly as something at the back of my mind told me I had forgotten something.

"Well, if you want, maybe we could catch an afternoon movie or something?"

"Sounds great, sure," I replied, still uncertain.

But she didn't appear to notice my hesitation, and replied, "Great. Have some toast and coffee."

After we both nibbled on the toast, we lay back on the bed and snuggled up. As we were chilling out, Paul burst in the door, as he always did, and said, "Hey, don't forget if you want to talk to me about your little mystery friend, let me know."

Ah, shit, I thought to myself. "Yeah, maybe later, thanks Paul." As Paul left, I mumbled to myself, "O'Connor's Café."

"What did you say?" Carly asked.

"Listen, I have to meet someone now, so can I meet up with you later?" I said sheepishly.

"Right now, really?"

"I know it's bad timing, but I have to meet someone important about a family matter," I said.

"Well, okay if you must," she said with a sigh. I got up and dressed as quickly as possible. Didn't even have time to brush my teeth – not that I had my toothbrush, and I would never use someone else's brush either.

"Sorry for running off like this, but this is important," I told Carly.

"No probs. I'll see you later anyway, right?" she asked.

"Definitely," I replied. I smiled at her and left the room. I shouted goodbye to the other two in the house and ran out the door and down the street.

Chapter 2
Revelations

WHILE STILL RUNNING, AND NOT fully focused, I ran straight into a man carrying two carry-out cups of hot coffee and sent them flying out of his hands and into the air.

"You fucking idiot!" he screamed in anger at me.

"I'm so sorry, I'm in a terrible hurry," I replied and kept going, with the man yelling abuse as I ran off in the distance.

I hailed a taxi and gave the driver the address. *Should be there on time*, I thought, looking at my watch. It was 10:49 a.m.

Pulling up outside the driver said, "That'll be eight euro fifty cents, please." Handing him a ten-euro note, I said, "Keep the change."

I got out and let out a big sigh; O'Connor's was right in front of me. I walked to the door and looked in through the glass window, and there he was. Looking at my watch it read 10:58 a.m. He looked up and saw me and gestured to come inside.

I walked in, immediately hit by the waft of coffee and cooking food, and headed for this mystery man, who said he knew my grandad. I had nothing to lose in just hearing what this mysterious Dr. Hoitdle had to say.

"Good morning, John, good to see you. I hope I didn't take you away from anything important?" he asked, as if he already knew where I had just come from.

"I was just with some friends overnight – but why do I think you already know that?" I replied.

"Please, won't you sit down?" He indicated the chair.

The waitress came over and placed a coffee in front of us both. "I took the chance you would be here and ordered for two," he said as he picked up the sugar.

"So, Dr. Hoitdle, are you going to explain what the hell is going on? I mean, how you know my grandfather, and why my father would lie about how he died?"

I added, "If I think you are lying to me, I'm walking out of here."

"Believe me, Mr. Ryan, I have no intention or interest in lying to you. Why would I?" he replied.

"Well, let's just see. Why don't you start from the beginning, and tell me what you know, and we'll take it from there?" I suggested. He nodded in agreement.

For the next twenty minutes, I sat and listened to the most incredible story I have ever heard or dared to believe.

He began, "The year was 1938, and Hitler had rounded up as many of the top scientists, engineers, mathematicians and physicists in Europe he could find and had them working on all sorts of weapons, scientific inventions, new technology. Under fear of the SS, he forced them to come up with anything that he could use against the future enemies of the Fatherland. Most of these men and women were forced, but some were German or Austrian, or Nazi sympathizers from France, Holland and even Poland. Your grandfather was lured over under the false pretences of a new breakthrough in creating a cure for cancer, as many were, and wanted to be involved, of course. Alas, they were held captive and made to work on weapons technology. I, too, was one of those scientists, and at twenty years old—not even graduated from technical science college in Berlin—I was a novice and looking to make my mark. Your grandfather had a degree in biochemistry and thought his skills were to be used for helping people, not destroying them. He was young like me, only twenty-three years old. He had studied in London and then moved to Germany in 1937 to pursue his dream of working with the top men and women of Europe.

"Anyway, one day one of the teams led by your grandfather was testing a new weapon deep in the Bavarian forests of Germany. It was revolutionary for its time. It involved electro-pulse magnification, which sent out a magnetic sound blast over a ten-mile radius and could destroy anything with electronics or mechanical engines. Enemy communications would crash, tank engines would stop, and, best of all, enemy fighter planes and bombers would fall from the skies. They were able to funnel the magnetic pulse so as not to destroy their own military assets, sending it out into the direction of where they needed.

"But in the midst of testing this remarkable machine, something else happened. Something they hadn't planned for. Something that could change the course of their upcoming war and of the world itself. The team had discovered this new machine created wormholes. They could bend time, my dear Mr. Ryan."

"Jesus. You're talking about time travel," I asked.

"Yes, the team, including your grandfather, had invented the greatest discovery of all time without even knowing it could happen. You cannot change what hasn't happened yet. But we believed we could change what *had* happened. So, we started testing it immediately. Reluctantly Hitler was informed of its capabilities, and, needless to say, he had these men and women put on full security protection. They spent the next two years running experiments, testing, failures, successes and many deaths. They were not allowed to leave their secret hideaway which was east of Berlin in an underground bunker, hidden on church grounds. That's where most of the preliminary work was done, and then we moved it to the testing site in Bavaria. Eventually on the 5th of September 1941 they successfully sent their first item back in time."

"Did it work?" I asked impatiently.

"Your grandfather sent a Nazi emblem pin to a specific point in time, exactly two years earlier—5th September 1939—just inside the perimeter fence of where they were housed. They all checked the area first to make sure it was clear, then went back inside and started the test. Once it was sent, they ran to the perimeter fence as fast as they could and there, they found the pin hidden in growth. Two years of fungi growth, rust and dirt covered the Nazi symbol, but you could make out its emblem. I cannot tell you how excited everyone was. Jumping up and down and hugging each other.

"The big problem now was how to avoid the Nazi henchmen coming in, taking over the project and causing mayhem," he finished.

"This sounds too incredible," I whispered.

With this, he took out a battered old pin and handed it to me. Looking down, I noticed the partial symbol of the Nazi emblem.

"Is this what I think it is?" I asked.

"Yes," he said.

"You've had it all this time?"

"Your grandfather gave it to me on the last day I ever saw him alive," he replied.

"What happened to him?"

"About two in the morning, we were sleeping in our bunks at the testing site in the Bavarian woods, when an air-raid siren sounded. We all got up and scuttled to a makeshift underground shelter. But I guess some of us were a little too late that night. A bomb hit our shelter just as we were at the entrance and sent everyone flying into the air. When I came around, I saw that the bunker around us had collapsed; I could see right up into the night sky. Guards were hurrying around trying to put out fires and help the wounded. Only two of our group survived: myself, of course, and your grandfather, but he only managed to survive the rest of the night. His last act was to give me this pin and he asked me to keep the machine safe and protect his family: your father, who was only a two-month-old baby, and your grandmother, who had moved with him to Berlin. Alas, I only managed to keep one of those promises."

"What do you mean?" I asked.

"The machine was moved back to Berlin. Back to the church and held there in secret. After Joseph passed away during the early hours in my arms, I was returned to Berlin a few days later under guard to check on any damage to our new creation. There was only me left to continue this work after that terrible night and I was hastily given a fresh batch of scientists and assistants to train. We were held there for the next few years working on getting it back in operation, but it was not going to plan," Hoitdle said sounding disappointed.

"Then what happened?"

"26th April 1945, the war was long-lost, and Hitler was days from committing suicide. I was summoned to Berlin headquarters – more like dragged from our secret bunker lab. I and a few of my assistants were working on some numerical equations when six SS guards burst in and ordered me out and onto a waiting truck. I was brought to a desperate place: Hitler's bunker. *The* bunker. As I was marched down those steps and into the deep narrow corridors, you could sense death was closing in. The sheer disbelief on some of the faces that it had come to this was harrowing to witness. That their great nation was on the brink of total destruction was just too much for some. Suicide was the only way out for many of the men and women in the bunker and across Berlin as the Russians closed in.

I was brought into an empty office and told to wait. Twenty-five minutes later, the door opened and in stepped Adolf Hitler with Joseph Goebbels by his side. The door was shut by an SS guard and they stood in silence staring at me. And then Hitler starting walking around the room, yelling that the war was far from over. He told me that we would lose this battle with the Russians in the next few days, but the war would be won years from now. It was up to me now, he told me.

I, of course, asked what he meant. It was then that I was given my orders. Goebbels gave me the important and top-secret assignment of putting together a team who could get the machine working again years from now when the time was right, to return to 1941 at the peak of Nazi power and start over where the same mistakes would not be repeated. Of course, I agreed but had no intention of making that happen. I had fallen out of love with Hitler and the Nazi propaganda that had ruined our people and our nation. But I did want the machine out of Nazi control, and I also feared it falling into Russian hands. So I agreed and was given a location on a map that only five people knew about. Hitler, Goebbels, two loyal SS guards, and an Austrian rocket scientist, who would help me in the future. This was where we were to bury the machine until it was ready to be resurrected. I took the map and their instructions and left them behind to their final downfall.

"We retrieved the machine from the church bunker, had it crated up and moved. It was driven to a location east of the city by the SS guards as far away from the battlefields as we could get. It was to be buried deep in a carefully chosen empty field. We had to be quick, as the Russians were only a few miles away and closing in fast. Ten Jewish slaves were brought in to help dig the massive hole. We dug all day and night. Once we got to ten feet deep, we lowered it down and covered it with a metal shield and filled the hole back in. I marked the coordinates of the field and put it in my pocket. The Jewish prisoners were put on a truck and I along with the Austrian scientist were ordered onto the truck. We drove away from the field as far as we could under Russian bombardment and eventually pulled up beside a burnt-out postal office.

"We were all ordered out and marched inside the building. The Jews were ordered up against a wall. I knew what was coming. They were machine gunned down with no mercy by the two SS guards. No one could know of the machine's existence. The SS guards turned to us and I can tell you I thought I was about to receive the same. But I had orders from Hitler, so surely I was safe?

"I was told to step away from the Austrian. You could imagine his face as he looked at me for help but all I could do is step aside and as he pleaded for help the two guards riddled him with bullets. One of the SS guards told me I was now the only one besides them who knew the location. But just as I was about to protest the shooting, they both bit down on cyanide pills and they dropped to the ground. I guess they had their orders from Hitler and were probably informed that their day would come again. I stood there for a while not knowing what to do. I heard gunfire and explosions closing in and decided I would try escape south from Germany across the border into Switzerland to try avoiding the oncoming Russian Red Army onslaught. If I couldn't make Switzerland, then I thought it was better to be captured by the Western Allies. Alas, I was cut off and eventually captured by the Russians five days later in East Berlin, hiding in the basement starving and cold with other terrified civilians and sent to a Russian prison work camp where I was held captive until 1951 when I was released. I got back to Berlin to discover that the Russians were now in control of East Berlin and I had no access to the machine.

"I visited the area with its buried secret many times, but communism held the city in its grip, and I thought I would never get the chance to retrieve our creation. Things got worse when construction of the Berlin Wall began in 1961, and I fled to the west.

"I had to abandon my plans for now. It was not until 1989 that I got a second chance to revisit that site — the fall of the Berlin Wall. The field was still there. It was now a cemetery.

"So, I assembled a crew and had them locate it with modern industrial metal detectors and found it under Mrs. Janus Staffel. Just as well we took the decision to bury it ten feet deep, otherwise it would have been found before then. So, we dug it up and shipped it out of Germany and held it in hiding until I could assemble the right team to test it once more. It took me eleven years to find the right people. People who I believed I could trust and who had the type of skills to bring it to life. But we kept hitting a snag, a snag I was not prepared for."

"Which was what?" I asked.

"No one could get it to work. They could get it to fire up, but it just wouldn't transport back in time. Two years later, my team finally worked out what the final piece of the jigsaw was. Your grandfather, you see, was a very clever man. He believed that the Nazis were far too radical, extreme and careless to possess and wield this type of power. So, he gave it a kind of password. that not even I knew about. Something we never worked out until 2002. Without this final piece, it's useless. He always suspected that the Nazis would assume control and do no end of damage to the world," Hoitdle eventually finished.

"What is this final piece you need?" I asked.

"You, Mr. Ryan," he said.

"What do you mean, me?" I demanded to know.

"I'm afraid that is something I cannot tell you here now, but if you come to Berlin to meet with my team, I can explain everything, and you can help us get our project back online."

"And why would you think that I would help you? If what you say is even possible, why on earth would I allow you to go back in time and give Hitler a second chance to win the War? Which he would, of course, given the information he would now control!" I retorted. "He would have a blueprint of every battle fought throughout the whole war and know every move of the Allies. Are you out of your fucking Nazi mind?"

Hoitdle sat back and let out a single laugh. "Do you really think that's what we are planning? It's a little more complicated and inventive than that, Ryan. I wouldn't help that bastard. That mass-murdering, brownshirt fascist destroyed Europe. No. Never. That's not what we want to do."

"So, what then? What will you do with this machine?" I asked.

"Come to Berlin with me tomorrow. I'll show you. You can meet the team and see for yourself. It's really quite remarkable, what we have planned. And if you don't like what we have to say, then you are free to go about your life as if we never met"

"And you'll let me," I said in a sarcastic voice.

"Yes, you have my word," he replied. He put his hand into his inner pocket and pulled out an envelope and placed it on the table. "In there, you'll find a ticket to Berlin, return of course, and expense money. If you come, you come. If not, have a good life, Mr. Ryan." As he stood up, he said, "I do hope you'll come see us Ryan. Shall we say goodbye, for now?" and walked out. I watched him until he was out of sight.

I picked up the envelope and saw the return ticket to Berlin was on Aer Lingus flight EI231, departing the following morning at 8:30. I pulled out the cash and counted out two thousand Euros. There was an additional piece of paper with a German Address: *Weisser Haus, Steinbecker, Route 158.* I gathered up the cash and tickets, put them in my inside pocket and left the café. As I headed home I kept a look out but saw no one suspicious.

"Do you think he'll come?"
"Oh, he'll come, don't you worry about that, Herr Doktor.*"*
"Did you tell him everything?"
"He knows enough for now. In good time, he'll understand the true extent of our plans and by then it will be too late."

Chapter 3
The Mansion

Arriving at Dublin Airport the next morning, I got the 8:30 flight out to Berlin. Sitting on the plane, I replayed yesterday's conversation in my head over and over. I also realized why my father told me that Grandad died in a car crash before the war – the great shame that would have engulfed the family at the time when it was discovered that he was working for the Nazis would have been a stigma that our family may never have overcome.

Following my meeting with Hoitdle, I had sat thinking for hours and hours, till I was interrupted by my phone ringing. Oh, shit, it was Carly, wondering where I was. I hadn't the guts to answer; I had forgotten about her. I sent a text. *'Carly, so sorry but something important came up and I have to go away for a while. See you soon. John.'*

'Yeah right, don't bother,' was her reply.

I felt bad.

Sitting on the plane I got the feeling of being watched again. I looked around and didn't see anyone I knew, but I couldn't shake the feeling. As we touched down in Berlin I started to get butterflies in my stomach.

I got off the plane and made my way to the arrivals gate. I had only packed an overnight bag and went through security without any hold ups. I was about to head to the taxi rank when I noticed a big man standing with a board with my name on it. I went over to him and said, "I'm John Ryan."

"Follow me I have a car waiting," he replied in a thick German accent. Without any further conversation, I followed him to a black BMW. He took my bag and threw it in the boot before opening the rear passenger side door to usher me in. "We have two-hour journey to Steinbecker, so just sit back and relax." He was mid-forties, stocky build, and had the look of one of those Stasi-type secret police officers from the days before the fall of the Berlin Wall; a don't-fuck-with-me type. His crew-cut hair was slightly greying, and his thick neck made it hard to turn his whole head around while speaking. His plain blue suit was so tight on him that if he moved suddenly, I felt it would burst open.

I just nodded, got in the car and sat back to take in the journey.

Arriving in the town of Steinbecker, I was getting antsy, wondering about what was ahead of me. We turned off Route 158 into a tree lined avenue, driving up a narrow road with overgrown hedges and bush. A minute later the road widened, and we pulled up in front of a large metal-gated entrance. The driver lowered his window and looked up at a camera pointing down towards the car. A few moments later the gate started to open slowly.

We drove in and, as I turned to look back, I saw the gates close behind us. I was looking around my new surroundings and noticed men walking German Shepherds by the perimeter wall, which seemed to wholly surround the grounds. The walls themselves must have been at least fifteen feet tall. Now I really was nervous. What were they guarding?

The driver, without turning around, curtly said, "We're here," as he pulled up in front of an old Victorian-style mansion. He got out, came to my rear door and opened it. I got out and waited while he got my bag out of the trunk. "This way."

I followed him up six wide concrete steps to the entrance and through the open doorway. As soon as I went inside, I heard a familiar voice.

"You made it, Mr. Ryan, I'm so happy."

"Good to see you too, Dr. Hoitdle. This is some place you have here," I said.

"Our little get-away for our like-minded friends; you know, somewhere to relax where prying eyes cannot interrupt," he said with pride. "Come, let me show me to your room, and then you can meet the team." He took my bag off the driver as he led me up a wooden winding staircase. Pictures of German landmarks, legends new and old, and what looked like expensive paintings, (not that I knew much about art) adorned the walls.

"I hope you're not too tired, John, from your trip," Hoitdle said.

"No, I'm fine, thank you," I replied.

"Good, I can't wait for you to meet everyone. I'm so excited, I'm like a child waiting for Father Christmas to arrive," he laughed. I just smiled back.

At the top of the stairs, we turned left and down a long corridor. There were closed doors along the way, which I assumed were other bedrooms.

"Who are we meeting?" I asked.

"Ah, here we are, this is your room," he interrupted. He led me inside and placed my bag on the bed. "We are all meeting for dinner at 6pm. You can relax and freshen up here after your long journey," he said. I looked at my watch; it was 2:45pm.

"Thank you – who are we meeting?" I asked again.

"Ah, the team, the people you will be working with…don't worry about them just now, *Herr* Ryan. Get comfortable, and I'll see you at six." He turned, walked to the door and closed it behind him.

I gazed around the room and took in my surroundings and then headed to the window. There I saw the guards again. It looked like the walls travelled the whole way around the mansion, reminding me of the Berlin Wall.

The room was very Victorian, with old wooden chairs and furniture. I went to the king-size bed and sat down on the edge running my hand over the quilted duvet. I let out a puff of air. *What the fuck am I doing here?*

I unpacked, trying to hang my clothing in the wardrobe with only two coat hangers. I thought to myself, *people don't stay here long*. I took a shower and dried off then lay on the bed and decided to nap for a while, setting the alarm on my watch to go off at 5:45pm.

I was awoken to my alarm and got up and got fully dressed. After refreshing my face and brushing my teeth in the bathroom, I looked at my watch and saw it was almost six. I splashed on a bit of aftershave and headed for the door. I went out into the corridor to discover one of the guards was waiting at the end of the hallway. "They're waiting for you," he said, pointing towards the stairs. I nodded and headed in the direction he'd indicated. Just then, a door opened across the hallway from my room and with a roar of "God damn it," out walked a raven-haired thing of beauty.

She looked at me and said, "Sorry about that, they won't let me make a phone call home." I just stared at her; she was so beautiful. "Well, I guess you must be the donor?"

"The donor?"

"Yes, you know," she made a needle in the arm gesture.

"I don't understand," I said.

"I'm Sara." She held out her hand.

"Hi, I'm John. John Ryan," I replied.

"Yes, I gathered that."

"They're waiting for you both," the grumpy guard said sternly.

"Oh, keep your hair on, we're coming," she shouted back at the guard, who looked a little taken aback. He was at least six feet two, and had a black security uniform on, radio on his belt on one side and a pistol on the other. The guard waited for us to take the stairs first and started to follow when we were halfway down.

I just smiled and followed Sara down the stairs, admiring her behind as she walked with total authority. She was about five feet eight, slim-build but not weak. Strong back, and firm thighs which showed through the tight-fitting black leggings she wore. Her black-heeled boots were shiny, and her grey wool top brought out the shape of her curves nicely. She had shoulder-length hair tied up in a ponytail. She had dark eyes and a dark complexion. Her accent was a mix of Italian and a hint of upper-class English, possibly educated in England as a child. She walked with an air of authority like she was used to getting her own way. She definitely made an impression on me from the start – she was truly stunning.

We made our way to the bottom, closely followed by the bulky guard. Passing through the sliding door on the left at the end of the stairs, I could hear a murmur of voices coming from the extended room further in.

"My god, would you look at this place?" Sara said, taking in her surroundings.

The room was of the 1940s, dated, but with some contemporary upgrades like the drinks bar and the darkened red curtains. The room was dominated by the wooden décor and the floral patterned-chairs looked like they were from the 1940s. I wasn't an expert, but it had that feel. Lamps were placed all around the room, with two large chandeliers hanging from the ceiling, about ten feet apart, drawing your gaze upwards.

"It sure is something," I replied.

"Ah, Mr. Ryan, and Sara, lovely as always," beamed Dr. Hoitdle as we entered the next room. Four other faces just stopped and starred at us as if waiting for a response.

"Hello," was all I could muster.

"What the fuck is all this about, Doc?" Sara bellowed, walking over and running her eye over all the other faces.

"Ha, don't you just adore her?" Hoitdle responded. "Come, let's sit, dinner will be ready soon. We have lots to discuss." We all sat down on the large comfy floral sofas and armchairs positioned around the room with Hoitdle in the middle, as we waited to hear our reasons for being here. "Let me introduce everyone to the group, and then we can all talk about why each of us is here. Okay? I should start with myself: I am Ralf Hoitdle, Doctor of Physics and Mathematics from the University of Berlin. To my left is Sara Letari, freelance photographer and Pulitzer prize winner, not just one, but for two years running. Sara is responsible for some of the world's most stunning shots both in the field of wildlife and well from all around the world. She also has the other side of the spectrum of those infamous shots of a certain President's assassination attempt, and many other brilliant once in a lifetime shoots." He spoke with such admiration – like a father would talk about his own daughter.

"That's me," Sara said flippantly with a wave of her hand.

"To Sara's left is cinematographer Eddie Hayes, American, with various awards in his home country for some of the best news shots to hit our TV screens. If something big is happening around the world, Eddie is there with his camera."

"Evening all," Eddie Hayes said in his New York accent while giving a cheap salute to the room. He seemed like a bit of a character.

Pointing to the next man in turn, Mr. Hoitdle continued, "This is Marko Hinterberg, Austrian communication and electronics expert. One of the best in his field."

The large stout man in his brown grubby suit and spotted tie just raised his glass of cognac in the direction of Hoitdle.

Pointing to his right, Hoitdle continued, "Next is Doctor Herbert Grundle. One of our top surgeons in Germany today, if I may say so," nodding knowingly towards the surgeon who nodded back in turn. He was a tall slim man with narrow facial features and brown stringy, slightly greasy hair; he dressed very smartly in a navy fitted suit, white shirt and red tie. Unusually for a doctor, he puffed away on a cigarette.

"Herbert has overseen some of the latest medical break-throughs in Germany and of course Europe over the last few years, and we are very grateful and honored to have him here and part of our team," continued Hoitdle.

The doctor just nodded once more and replied back, "The honour is all mine, Doctor Hoitdle."

"Some of you have met Hermann Leitman, our head of security." Hoitdle pointed to the man who had picked me up at the airport. *Figures*, I thought to myself.

"Oh, the ape you mean," Sara quipped. The stocky German just shuffled in his seat and said nothing.

"Now, now Sara, please, let's not get personal," Hoitdle reprimanded her. She just smiled away to herself and sat back into the sofa. "If I may continue – lastly, we have John Ryan, research assistant to Professor Hartley at the biggest university in Dublin. And if I may go further, future professor in his own right," Hoitdle said pointing in my direction.

"Thank you, Doctor Hoitdle," I felt obliged to reply.

"So, that's our little group. And now you want to know why we are all here, I'm sure. Why this group?" He looked around at each of us.

Just then a tall slim man in a penguin suit, who I assume was the butler, appeared from another set of sliding doors to announce that dinner was being served.

"Ah, good, I'm sure you are all hungry for answers, but let's sort out our hungry appetites first," Hoitdle said in a jovial manner.

We all were ushered into the next room through the sliding doors. I saw a long, beautiful dining table, covered lavishly with food and wine. I must admit my mouth was watering with anticipation.

I noticed table seating cards and began looking for mine.

"I believe you are sitting next to me, John," said Sara. I paused for a second and went around the table to join her, where I noticed the place card had Eddie Hayes name on it.

"Em… I think that place is for Eddie," I said, regretfully.

"Not anymore," she replied quickly and took the card and threw it under the table before anyone saw. I looked at her sheepishly, shrugged and sat down. "Americans are so loud and arrogant don't you think?" she followed.

"Some are, I guess," I replied, hoping no one overheard us. Too late.

"Nonsense, Sara, some of us actually are loud, arrogant, handsome and great in bed too. You should know." It was Eddie Hayes.

"In your dreams," Sara quipped back.

Eddie just laughed it off and sat down in the place with no name card. "I'll just sit here, I guess." Eddie looked over and smiled at me. He was a slightly overweight man with a mop of thick black curly hair. He was clean-shaven, and his clothes spoke of no sense of style whatsoever: corduroy trousers, multi-coloured shirt and navy jacket. His shoes were plain black loafers. A total mess. He was a native New Yorker and typically loud and opinionated. He must have been in his mid-thirties, very arrogant, but I also found him funny. He had a wife back home who he only saw every so often. It appeared to be a mutual arrangement and it allowed Eddie to travel the world for his work.

Once all the invited guests had sat down, Doctor Hoitdle had the house staff begin their duties of filling wine glasses, bringing food in and out and scurrying around us like house servants from an era past. I was starving and I tucked into a beautiful starter of smoked salmon on a bed of cucumber and freshly chopped dill, and drank what I just found out was a very expensive wine, a 1934 Château Lafite Rothschild. Doctor Hoitdle took great pleasure in telling his guests that it had come up from his cellar, and it seemed to impress Sara.

"Wow, Doctor Hoitdle, you are truly spoiling us tonight," she said. I had to assume it was a very good wine. Sara picked up her glass and turning to me, we clinked glasses. "Here's to odd new friends," she giggled. I just repeated, "To odd new friends" and looked at her for a few moments.

As the four-course meal was nearing the end, and after some long drawn-out small talk between the guests, Doctor Hoitdle ordered his servants to clear the tables as we returned to the living room where we first all met. Everyone retook their original seats and stopped talking, just sitting back, watching each other. After a few more moments of hustling and bustling around the staff eventually left the room.

And then Doctor Hoitdle began speaking.

"Friends, distinguished guests and fellow colleagues," he began. "We are on the verge of an historical breakthrough. One of magnificent splendour, one of unprecedented, unchartered and terrifying endeavours in the history of mankind". He paused for a moment, as if to allow the tension to rise, and then he continued.

"One of the most defining and momentous eras of our past was that of the events, leading to, during, and after World War Two. Many people study, argue, debate, and write about what happened during those deadly years, but more fundamentally, what would have happened if Germany had won the war. If Hitler and his armies had managed to hold the Russians at Stalingrad and Moscow. Yes, maybe the Americans would have used the bomb on Germany which was planned before it was eventually used on Japan. That surely would have ended the war in Europe right there. But maybe Germany could have held on and developed the bomb themselves and then it was a whole new ball game, as you Americans say. With Russia neutralized, the Germans could have re-deployed massive troop and armoured support to the west to combat the American-led allies before the bomb was ready to be deployed in 1945.

"Each battle had its own consequence. The African corps with Rommel eventually lost due to lack of reserves and fuel which slowed his push to end Montgomery when he had them on the run.

"Every battle won or lost had a knock-on effect that affected the overall outcome of the war. In the end, Germany was fighting on too many fronts. But the question still stands. What if Hitler had won? What would be the shape of Europe and indeed the world today if Germany was the victor? Would we have seen a truce in the west? Probably. Russia in the hands of German control. As victor, would Hitler have been viewed and written about as a mad man intent on just conquering the world and exterminating all the

Jews? Would we even know about the Holocaust? Would we care? Yes, perhaps. I know it seems cold and harsh, but how many people today or in this room think and care too much about the victims of other conquerors like Napoleon, Alexander the Great and the great Roman Empire? Why? Because it's all in the past, they won, and we glorify it. Why not Hitler? Because he lost and lost badly. So, the victors get to write about him anyway they like." At this point, I thought to myself, *Hoitdle could be quoting right out of my Two Sides college submission.* Hoitdle continued, "And rightly so. That's the price you pay. But under a truce with the Americans, if Hitler had been winning ultimate victories in fortress Europe and taking Russia's vast oil and food supplies under German control, do you think America, Britain, or any other European country would be writing about this mad Austrian who had so much hatred for the Jews? No, I don't think so. So, my friends, here we are. Why all the drama? Well…what if we could answer these questions? What if we could see for ourselves – know for sure what happens when Hitler wins the war—"

Eddie Hayes interrupted him. "Hang on a minute, what do you mean when you say *'when'* Hitler wins the war?"

"Just that, Eddie," Hoitdle replied. "Today, here, right now you are all about to re-write history: not just read or write about it, but *make* it.

"How is that possible, Doctor Hoitdle?" I asked.

"I'm glad you asked, Mr. Ryan," Hoitdle said looking right at me. "Five years ago, here in our discreet laboratory we had our first breakthrough. We sent back our first test project and recovered it just out there in the woods. A little rusty, I must say, but none the less intact, and sixty-two years older. I have it here in my pocket if you want to see." Hoitdle put his hand in his pocket and pulled out what looked like an old coin; it was the same pin he had shown me back in Dublin. A 1936 Reichsparteitag badge, a pin made for the annual Nazi party rallies held in Nuremberg during Hitler's reign. It obviously meant a lot to him.

"What do you mean, you sent it back and recovered it?" Eddie asked with a tone of disbelief.

"Eddie, you know why we are here. We sent it back in time. Back to 1941 and recovered in 2002."

We all looked at each other for a while. While Eddie, Sara and I knew why we had been brought here, we still had serious doubts that Hoitdle and his goons were really trying to sell this time travel story. It felt like they were in fact on a different planet than the rest of us, yet to deliver anything other than tall stories. Yet despite our nervous laughter, his faithful followers had remained calm with impassive facial expressions.

"Do you want to see how it works?" Dr. Hoitdle interrupted. We stopped laughing and waited. "Come, follow me. If proof is what you need, then proof is what you shall have." He stood up to leave the room and we all followed.

Chapter 4
Meeting BETI

We followed the Doctor out of the room and into the main hallway where I first met Hoitdle in the mansion. We continued to follow him down a long corridor to the left of the main staircase and he stopped at the end as if he were leading school kids into their next lesson. At the end of the corridor we stopped and waited while he unlocked a narrow wooden door. He went through and clicked on a light switch. "Come through," he beckoned. As he continued, we all went in one by one, where we discovered a staircase leading down in a spiral. It felt cold and damp.

At the end Hoitdle was waiting for us. "From this point on, what you are about to see is top secret. You are never to repeat what you have seen to anyone outside of this group. Remember, we know everything about all of you." He took the time to look at each of us individually. We all knew what he meant. We all had families and friends that could be gotten to. "I'm sure it won't come to that" he added.

In front of us was a large steel door with an electronic code pad which Hoitdle entered the number 200489. "This password can be used for now by all of you," Hoitdle said.

"Interesting," I said out loud.

"What is interesting, Mr. Ryan?" Hoitdle asked.

"The code, it's the birth date of Hitler," I replied.

"Very astute of you, Mr. Ryan. Let's go in, shall we?"

Eddie leaned in close to me and said, "Hitler's birthday, really. Cute, very cute."

The door unlocked and Hoitdle pushed the heavy door open to reveal a large open room with a vast array of electronic and computer equipment surrounding the room. At the very far end of the room stood a large, steel, dome-shaped structure. Three men in white coats were already in there busying around with clipboards and hardly took notice as if they already knew to expect us.

"Come in, come in, don't be afraid," Hoitdle said all excited. "This is where the magic takes place. This is where all of you will witness and take part in the greatest achievement man has ever known."

"And women. Don't forget us women, Doctor Hoitdle," Sara said with a sneer.

"Indeed, forgive me, Sar,a" Hoitdle added with a smile.

"Is this what you and your little white-coated friends are planning to use to go back in time?" Eddie Hayes said with a touch of sarcasm, pointing at the dome.

"Yes." One word from Hoitdle.

Eddie shrugged and walked over to the dome.

"It's called a Bio-Electromagnetic-Time Inducer or as we like to call her.... BETI. A bit of a mouthful, I think."

"BETI will do fine for me," Sara quipped.

"Ha, yes," Hoitdle chuckled.

"Are you really trying to tell us this thing actually works?" I said with uncertainty. I in fact did not know what to believe.

"Why don't we give you a little demonstration?" Hoitdle said. "Your watch is a family heirloom, is it not? Handed down from your grandfather, to his son, and then you?"

"How did you know that?"

"There isn't much I don't know about you all," he retorted. "Your watch, if I may."

Reluctantly I took it off and handed it over. "Please be careful with it," I insisted.

"But of course, I promise your watch will be perfectly safe." Changing to a stronger tone and demeanor Hoitdle turned to his white-coated minions and instructed them "Begin the sequence".

He took my watch over to a cabinet, removed a small metal case and placed my watch inside. Closing it, he walked over to the dome and entered a code we could not see, and a rounded door opened outwards. Hoitdle walked inside as we all followed him around to see inside. He placed the box containing my watch on the metal floor. In fact, the whole inside was a single round, steel-plated room. He stepped back outside and closed the door by punching in the code. The door locked.

"Enter coordinates. One hundred feet lateral, one-foot horizontal below and sixty-two years," Hoitdle told one of his white-coats. White-coat did as he was instructed on his computer, and with that a warning alarm sounded all around us. "Twenty seconds to initiation, Dr. Hoitdle," the white-coat relayed.

"What's happening?" Eddie Hayes questioned.

"History, my good man," Hoitdle responded. "Wait and see."

Ten seconds to initiation. The dome started humming, the noise level growing. It was like the sound of an airplane plummeting from the skies. "Five seconds, four, three, two, one— Initiate," the white-coat said. What sounded like a suction noise was heard coming from the dome, and then an eerie pause. Then suddenly.... Boom! A deafening sound like a lightning strike screamed from the dome and we all jumped in fright. My heart was racing. Everyone stood very still, silent and waited with open mouths.

After a short pause Hoitdle said, "It's back."

"What's back?" I said.

"Why, your watch, of course", Hoitdle declared.

"In the dome, you mean?" I asked.

"No, no. It would not be safe there for sixty-two years, especially as it would be buried under this house" he said. "Go upstairs and out into the rear garden. Go to the wall at the end of the garden and you'll find a tall pillar marked with an X on one side. Stand with your back to it and walk one hundred metric feet dead ahead and dig one foot down. There you will find your watch. Oh, and take a shovel with you, you'll get one in the garden shed on your way down there. Good luck."

"Yeah, good luck on a wild goose chase," Eddie Hayes quipped.

"I'll come with you," Sara said and followed me towards the door. "I have to see this for myself."

The steel door was opened for us by one of the white-coats, and we hurried back out and up the spiral staircase until we turned towards the kitchen and out of the door into the back garden. It was dark out and very little light was coming from the back of the mansion. We spotted the shed, just as Hoitdle had said, and pulled opened the door and looked around inside until we spotted the shovel.

"Hey, grab that lamp too," Sara ordered. I grabbed the lamp and Sara lit it up with a lighter she had in her pocket. She picked up the shovel and closed the door behind me. We headed towards the wall at the end of the garden and saw the tall pillar. Sara leaped onto the wall and stepped down onto the ground on the other side to examine the pillar. "Well, here's the X," she said.

"Okay, this is getting too weird," I added.

"I think it's going to get a little weirder if we find your watch, don't you think?" she replied.

"Yeah, I guess," I said.

Looking out into the woods, I lifted the lamp up to try see what we were heading for, but couldn't see further than a few feet.

"Okay, one hundred feet, let's count," Sara said, already with her back to the X. "I'll stay right behind you," I said. We made our way out steadily and passed what could have been freshly dug areas of dirt. We kept going steady until we reached ninety-eight feet when Sara stopped and said, "Did you hear that?"

"What?" I said, trying not to look or sound scared. "What did you hear?"

"Wait," she said. We both waited a few moments and then she finally said, "Sorry, maybe it's my imagination; thought I heard something out there. Don't worry about it."

"Okay," I said gingerly.

"Ninety-nine, one hundred – okay, I guess this is it," she confirmed.

"Here, hold the lamp and I'll start digging," I said. She took the lamp and held it over the spot where I was now digging. The soil didn't feel loose so I guessed this was a fresh dig. The night was cold, and you could see our breath by the light of the lamp. Five minutes into digging, I hit something hard. I slowed down and dug around whatever I had just hit.

"Is that it?" Sara inquired.

"I'm not sure, give me a minute," I replied. I dug out a little more dirt around the item until I could manoeuvre it free. "Got it." Dropping the shovel, I bent down on one knee and leaned in and pulled up a steel box covered in dirt. I looked up at Sara and she stared back at me.

"Go ahead, open it up," she said softly. She knelt beside me and I looked at the box. It only had a clip that needed to be pulled open. I opened it up towards me. We both stared inside and took a breath. There it was: my grandfather's watch. "No fucking way," she said. "How did he do that?"

I took the watch out and read the back. It was definitely my watch alright. It read 'to the future and our past'.

I now knew what that meant.

"Come on, let's get back and find out just what the hell is going on with this machine and what Hoitdle and his goons have planned for the past," I said.

"And what he wants with us, too," Sara added.

"Yeah. But I think I already know," I sighed in reply.

We made our way back to the mansion and found everyone had returned to the living room.

They all just stared at me, waiting for me to reveal what some of them already knew. I paused, then held up my watch.

Hoitdle just smiled at me; he already knew it would be there. Eddie Hayes walked over to me and asked to see the watch. "What is this, some kind of magic trick? You probably switched it when we were down in Frankenstein's basement when no one was looking, and had someone bury it," he claimed.

"How?" I shouted. "When? In the space of ten minutes you think they switched my watch, gave it to someone who ran out into the woods in the dark and buried it one hundred feet out and then was somehow able to fill in the hole with dirt and make it look like the area was never dug up before?" I ended my rant.

"Maybe," Eddie Hayes replied with doubt now in his voice as he turned and headed for the drinks bar and poured himself a drink from the nearest open bottle which happened to be a Bourbon.

"So, now do you believe what we can do?" Hoitdle asked.

"Yes," I replied.

"Good; then you are ready to take the next step and begin our historic journey into the past to see what the future would have been," Hoitdle proclaimed.

"Why this?" Sara interrupted.

"Why what?" Hoitdle asked.

"Why Hitler, Germany, changing this past, why *this*? Why give evil a chance, a life? What are you trying to do here exactly?" she demanded.

"Why not?" Hoitdle retorted. "Isn't this one of the greatest questions of our time? I say, let's answer it."

"How?" I asked. "How can you help Hitler win?"

"We will go back and offer him the information about every major battle lost during the war. From 1941, Hitler will win every battle his armies engage in, because he and his Generals will have history on their side – literally. When to attack. When to hold. How many soldiers needed. The Allies' weaknesses. We will eliminate the scientists who made the atom bomb for the Americans. Let's make it a fair war, I say," he joked.

"Well, even if that could be done, why the hell would we help you achieve this sick demented plan to give Hitler his glory? We won't allow you get away with it," Sara insisted.

"Oh, my dear Sara, I think you have misread my intentions here," Hoitdle replied. "Let me explain the full extent of what we plan to do. Firstly, I couldn't agree more. Hitler was an evil a crazed madman hell bent on destruction and I hated too for that, just like you. But what we plan is merely a documented diary of what the world would have been like after the war, and the many years following it. And today, of course, if he had won. Your team will go back and document every aspect of life from 1941 to present day, dropping in and out of different times, recording everything in sheet, in photos and in film. Then, when we have completed our recorded works, we will go back and reverse the past back to what we know today."

"You can do that?" I inquired. Everyone looked to see Hoitdle's reply.

"Yes, John, we can do that," Hoitdle said reassuringly. "But that's for tomorrow. It's late and it's been a long day. Why don't we retire for the night and begin first thing after breakfast? Let's say 8 a.m. sharp, yes?" Hoitdle requested with authority.

"I want to know more now," Eddie interrupted.

"Oh, I know you do, Eddie, and I'm sure you all do, but we have a lot more to discuss and show you and it is quite late, so if you wouldn't mind leaving it for tonight, we can all get a good night's sleep and begin again tomorrow, please," Hoitdle finished.

We all nodded in agreement and started to make our way out of the room towards the stairs leading back to our rooms. Sara walked ahead of me and again I was treated to her lovely rear as she ascended the staircase. With a knowing look, over her shoulder I got a sense she was checking to see if I was admiring the view. We reached the top of the stairs and this time there was no guard loitering at the top. We headed down the corridor and Sara arrived at her door and turned as I approached and paused in front of her.

"Well – that's a lot to take in, don't you think?" she said.

"It sure is," I replied.

"Good night John. I'll be here if you need to discuss anything maybe, if you want to, or not, well, sleep well," she said, stumbling over her words.

"You too, Sara, have a good night," I replied with ease.

Just then, Eddie arrived in the hallway and he walked to the first bedroom on the left which backed onto mine. He looked down at us and shouted down, "Night night, travellers!"

"Goodnight Eddie," we both replied in quick succession. He went in and closed his door behind him.

"Okay, sleep well," Sara said entering her room, slowly closing the door behind her, smiling at me as the door shut.

I crossed the hallway to my room and went inside and closed the door behind me. I paused for a moment thinking about Sara, then walked to the bed, sat down and kicked off my shoes. I fell back onto the bed and lay there for a while trying to take everything in. Was is possible? Was it ethical? Was I really contemplating the possibility of going back in time and changing the course of World War Two to assist in turning Germany from the most hated country of that time to a superpower with a vast empire resulting in the deaths of millions of people and enslaving so many more? Could Hoitdle then really turn it all back – and could we record all this and bring it back to present day? If history is changed, doesn't that then affect the future? We could end up back in a different future. If we give Hitler victory, could we end up changing so much that we lose control, and BETI never gets created and we end up in a world of Nazi German supremacy, unable to escape? What if Hitler gets his hands on this technology as the final victor? What would he do with it? Go back further and change World War One? The butterfly affect would be catastrophic, and that was what scared me the most. So much planning, so much depended on total secrecy and precision. It was so overwhelming and really all too much to take in and digest.

I needed to sleep, and I drifted off pondering my fate.

Chapter 5
Early Departure

"John, John, wake up," Sara yelled, as I woke up from a deep sleep. She was standing over me and tapping me lightly on the face. "Something's happened; we all need to meet downstairs now." I was still half asleep and looked over at the clock on the bedside locker. 6:30 a.m.

"What's going on?"

"Hoitdle wants us all downstairs, right now, let's go," she repeated.

"But can't you just tell me now?" I replied, still in the same position and the same clothes from a few hours ago that I'd fallen asleep in. I was stiff and sat up gingerly.

"No time, I'll explain all when you come down," she said and hurried back out the door. I heard her footsteps fade away down the corridor.

I quickly went into the ensuite bathroom, ran the tap and threw water on my face. I grabbed my toothbrush and gave my teeth a quick once then grabbed a change of clothes from the overnight bag I had brought from Dublin and changed as quickly as I could. Looking around the room, I sensed it would be the last time I would be here. I breathed a deep sigh and left the room and headed downstairs. As I neared the bottom, I could see people dashing around and coming and going through the coded entrance to the underground cellar where the time machine was. I made my way into the large open living room where we had our first meeting and saw Eddie Hayes sitting down typing frantically into his laptop.

"What's going on?" I asked.

"We're ramping up our plans – or their plans, I should say," he replied.

"What does that mean, ramping up plans—"

"It means get your hat, coat and identity papers, Mr. Ryan. I think we're all going for a long ride in BETI," he replied.

"Hang on, where's Doctor Hoitdle?" I demanded.

"Where do you think?" Eddie replied, looking down at the wooden floor while banging his heel on it at the same time.

I headed towards the back corridor that lead to the cellar door and ran into Sara making her way there with various pieces of photography equipment strewn over her shoulders.

"Crazy around here, isn't it?" she declared. The doorway was open, and I let Sara go through first. We headed down the spiral stairs and I was greeted by excited and busy white-coats, along with Hoitdle, Marko Hinterberg and Herbert Grundle barking out orders to anyone in the room. I was about to ask what the hell was going on, when Hoitdle spotted me.

"Mr. Ryan! Good; you're here, we can begin. Did you sleep well?" he asked.

"Yeah, sure, all of four hours," I retorted.

"Sorry about that, but we have to move everything forward," he replied. My head started to spin, with the movement and noise of chattering white coats speaking in German and computers humming, BETI's warning alarm and the bright lights of the cellar. I could feel it coming I could feel hysteria building and boiling up in the lower depths of my stomach as I tried to stay focused on a visual point of reference, trying to stop the room spinning faster and faster. I spun around, looking for a way out, looking for intervention, for anything. I put my hands on my face and crouched down and after a few moments I erupted, "STOP!"

The people in the room stopped in their tracks and stared in my direction. They all waited for Hoitdle's reaction.

I spoke. "Just stop for one moment, will you? Jesus, what the fuck is going on? Doctor Hoitdle, why are we doing this now? And why do you think I'm—or any of us for that matter—even considering going along with this insane plan of yours that may not even work? What if we can't get back or we are unable to change anything or what if we change too much?" I couldn't stop. "I'm not ready, you're not ready, I need more information, and I need more time to think. I just arrived yesterday, and you want me to get into a machine that may send me sixty-two years back in time, or worse, may just send me into a box in the ground outside for all I know, and for what? For our amusement. Our speculation. It was just a paper. It was a stupid college project on 'what if'. That's all. What are we doing here? We are on a dangerous path from which we may never recover or understand, yet you and your goons are jumping right in without fear that it will work, and work without fail."

I had stopped and I only now noticed that everyone had fallen silent, including the noise of the machines.

"Leave us alone, would you please?" Hoitdle asked.

There was a slight pause, then the white-coats, along with Hinderberg, all started heading out towards the stairs. Sara put her last piece of equipment on the floor, looked at me reassuringly, and followed the men out. I sat down on a chair by the wall and bowed my head.

"Well, you've been holding that in for a while," Hoitdle chuckled. I looked up at him and let out a mild laugh and followed with, "I guess I have."

Hoitdle retrieved a chair and parked it in front of me and sat down. He paused a moment and then reached out his right hand and patted me a few times on the knee. I took my hands away from my face and looked at him as he tilted his head. He had a warm smile which seemed odd on him and after a moment he began to speak.

"Your grandfather was a great man, a man with insight, real genius and a keen sense of righteousness. Like someone else I know," he said, looking at me. I smiled at Hoitdle and sat back up in my chair. He continued, "When your grandfather first realized what we had developed, he knew all too well how lethal it could become in the hands of the wrong people. Including Hitler, even though he was working for Germany at the time. He was forced to build these weapons, you know, just like many of his colleagues. So, he started working on a way to keep the Nazis from using it for their destructive ways. He knew he had to protect the world from such a destructive power. If the SS got their hands on this working technology, they could destroy the world as we know it. So, he came up with a secret formula to start the machine that no one could understand, except for one or two other close colleagues he could trust – people brought in from outside Germany, unsympathetic to the Nazi cause. A Swiss biochemist, and I think maybe a French chemist…It was such a long time ago. But even they didn't know how to administer the exact formula without your grandfather's guidance. It wasn't until five years ago that we knew what your grandfather had done."

"Tell me, Doctor Hoitdle – what formula? What had he done?" I asked him.

"Well, you see John, your grandfather mixed his blood—his DNA—into the mixing fluid that starts the initial sequence. An early bio-technology inception, if you will, probably the first of its kind. Without his blood, the time machine cannot start. Ingenious, wasn't it?" he exclaimed.

"It was," I agreed.

"Like a password on a computer today," Hoitdle continued. "Un-hackable, of course, unless you had strands of his DNA. But of course, he was long since dead and his remains never recovered. I think he planned it that way."

"So how did you manage to get the machine going without his blood?" I asked.

"It turns out family members have similar DNA strands that can be formulated into the mixing fluid which allows us to bypass the original strands. We need those similar DNA strands," Hoitdle said.

"Ah, you mean me," I said. "Did you ever try to get blood from my Father?"

"We tried, John, but it did not work. It was unfortunate that sometimes the strands are not strong enough. But someone else's in that family line was," he said, and then paused looking right into my eyes.

"But I never gave you my blood," I said questioningly.

"No, not knowingly you didn't," Hoitdle said sheepishly.

"You stole my blood? How…when, where?" I demanded to know.

"Do you remember about six years ago; you were knocked down by a car while out on your bicycle? You were brought to the hospital with a broken right arm and a large cut to your lower left leg. A lot of blood loss, I remember." Hoitdle paused.

"Yes, I remember. What, you somehow managed to get hold of my blood? How exactly? Did you have people watching me?" Hoitdle just looked at me. "Jesus, you did have people watching me."

"I'm afraid so. After the failure of your father's DNA, you became very important to our plans. You were our last hope. We managed to get a blood sample, yes, stolen from your ward by our good friend Hermann Leitman and had it flown out here for testing," Hoitdle said.

"Oh, that big lump," I quipped.

"John, you wouldn't believe the excitement when it worked. Seeing it come to life – I remember it was a very cold, bitter December in 1997, and we had been testing different amounts of your blood droplets all day and we had almost packed it in for the night, when we got the breakthrough we had been waiting for. We had pretty much used all of your sample so you can imagine how excited we were to see BETI come to life. We tested her, and it worked just like the pin I showed you in Dublin. It was a bitterly cold night, I remember, but my heart was warm with pride. So, after that, we patiently waited nearly six years to find the right team and formulate what we feel is a foolproof plan to ensure the utmost success. So, here we are, Mr. Ryan. Here we are, at the crossroads of history. And one you can be a big part of. If you truly want it," Hoitdle enthused.

"Why do you still need me then, if BETI is already working for you?" I asked.

"Well, we know how much passion and expertise you have on that explosive period, so it was really a case of killing two birds with one stone, if you will. We need your blood to keep mixing the formula, John. It only works for so long and then it weakens. We need fresh blood samples for each time we programme a jump. So, that's why you are really here, John. Now you know the full truth." Hoitdle got up from his chair and walked over to his creation and lovingly ran his hand slowly over its steel casing, like a jockey caressing his horse. He turned and looked at me.

"Well, Mr. Ryan, are you ready to live your grandfather's work, to explore what no human could ever think possible? To answer all the questions you've been looking to get answered all your life? But if you are, I need to warn you, we need to move fast, as certain outside forces are getting suspicious of our activities and may poke their noses in where they do not belong. It could shut us down, hence our need for expediency."

I looked up at Hoitdle, walked over to meet him at the dome, paused and took a gulp. I stared into the open doorway of BETI and after a few moments I turned to the doctor and nodded twice. He nodded back, smiled, put his hand on my shoulder and walked away towards the doorway to give his team the good news they had been waiting for.

Chapter 6
1941 Preparations

AND SO IT BEGAN: THE team assembled, instructions given, everyone knew their roles.

I was to be sent back to 1941 as a Nazi sympathizer – an Irishman who wanted to make contact with the Germans to offer vital information on English military intelligence and to gain access to better weapons. But my true goal was to infiltrate the German High Command, pass their security and somehow gain access to Hitler's supposedly impenetrable command centre to try convincing him and his henchmen to believe my secret: that I had information that would win the war for Germany. How I was going to do that was still an overwhelming obstacle I couldn't yet see a way around.

Sara and Eddie's instructions were to document, film and photograph as much as they could in the heart of Nazi-occupied Europe, using our latest camera technology and video equipment disguised within old camera materials from 1941. *Yeah, sure, no problem*, I thought. They were to go in the guise of an Italian photographer employed by an Italian national newspaper, with Eddie as Sara's assistant mute husband who relied on his wife for communication. The idea behind his being 'mute' was to avoid his speech being heard by any suspicious ears, who could notice his American accent and give them up to the Gestapo. The thought of Eddie as a mute amused everyone, except him of course. Sara's supposed brief was to be to capture German and Italian splendour so she could show the world the great German-Italian empire in all its glory, in the form of pictures and words, from the war days to the final outcome of the war so future generations would be able to see history as it happened. She could use her own name in counterfeit 1941 identity papers, as she was named after her grandmother from Milan so if they traced the name back it would show no discrepancies. Eddie was the tricky one, as Sara's grandmother was a widow—her grandfather had died in 1939—so they were unable to use his name on forged papers. They came up with a simple solution: Eddie was a mute from an orphanage, had no family, making it easier to explain his lack of both education and information. So he became Toti Letari. He took his wife's name, as the orphanage never knew who his parents were, and just knew him as Toti. They met while Sara was visiting Milan in 1935 when she walked into a baker's shop to buy some bread where he worked as a back-room baker. When they saw each other, they were immediately smitten. They soon started dating and fell in love with their mutual love of photography and art. He soon left the baker's and travelled the world with Sara to photograph the world as her assistant. That was the short, simple story they were to stick to if questioned. If they were arrested and tortured during an interrogation, who would believe their real story anyway? Europe 1941 was a scary place to be for anyone unsympathetic to the Third Reich. They were always going to be in danger, but for these two this was outweighed by the excitement of capturing on film one of the most incredible pieces of history in our time.

As for me, how would I be able to get myself standing in front of the leader of the Nazi party, Adolf Hitler? *Let's assume for one moment Hoitdle can pull this off, and send us back in time to 1941, and I can travel freely in occupied Europe, make my way to where Hitler's headquarters lay deep on the eastern front of Prussia, through many checkpoints, through three perimeter levels of high SS security and into the bunker, the Wolf's Lair, where Hitler's planning his decisive battle with the Russians, Operation Barbarossa.* I was starting to feel very anxious and uneasy about this crazy plan; and whether, most of all, I could trust these people.

Just as I was reading over my instructions, Hermann Leitman, head of security, walked in.

"Ah, there you are, Leitman, you have them, good, good," said Hoitdle.

Without saying a word, the burly man handed Hoitdle an envelope; he nodded to the doctor and without pausing, gave me a glaring glance, and turned and left. "Here are your identity papers to help you get to Prussia," Hoitdle said, passing me the envelope.

I walked over to one of the metal desks and removed the contents of the envelope. "That's twenty thousand marks, all legit printed from 1938. That should be enough to get you by and maybe pay off anyone that needs to be, so to speak," Hoitdle said. "About $35,000 in today's money." And, of course, my new identity papers: an IRA recruit sent to contact the Nazis with orders to buy weapons and to aid in the fight against the English occupation of Northern Ireland in exchange for Allied military intelligence. Quite plausible, I thought, as Germany had looked to using the IRA during the war to help cause mayhem on the English home front to distract them from the war with Germany. "Patrick O'Reilly from Dublin," I said out loud. "Shouldn't be too hard to pull off the accent."

"Ha, no, just what *we* thought, Mr. Ryan," Hoitdle replied. "Well, I think everything is in order. We'll start our preparations, unless you need anything else?" I shook my head and Hoitdle turned to speak with his white-coated minions to prepare for our incredible journey.

And so, the last plans were finalized.

It was predicted that if the Nazis accepted my ludicrous idea, they would defeat the Russians within six months, and the war would be over. They would have to contact the team of 1941 and meet the young Doctor Hoitdle, explain everything to him to then have him transport us all back to 2003 and back to the mansion with the documented films and evidence of the world under a Nazi-controlled Europe. Five different jumps were to be made: 1941, 1943, 1946, 1950 and 1975, spending three months documenting in each time zone. While Sara and Eddie would be aging in normal time, each time they jumped back in time they would be meeting an older Hoitdle.

I had only one mission: to convince the Nazis in 1941 to follow our outlandish plans to win the war. Once the war was over; I was to return to 2003 and my mission would be over – or so I was led to believe.

So, you made him understand. Now we can make our final preparations as planned. Everything is starting to fall into place. Excellent work, Doctor, excellent work indeed.

Chapter 7
Arrival

Standing in front of BETI, I felt my heart fluttering like a captured butterfly. My legs were jelly, I could all but hold myself steady; that is, until I felt my right hand being clutched and held tight by Sara's soft hand. Looking up towards me, she smiled and nodded once, and turned to look at this monstrous creation that stood beckoning us. I too turned my head to look at this gleaming death trap, closed my eyes, took a long deep breath and exhaled. Opening my eyes, I stared once more into the abyss and with determination tried to face my fears. I held my gaze, as if I could intimidate BETI.

Sara looked at me once more and with raised eyebrows said, "Ready?" With a slight pause, I turned to her and replied, "Ready."

With trepidation and excitement combined, we slowly started to move in tandem towards our destiny, all the while holding tight onto Sara's hand till we reached BETI's entrance. I feared what the future held for us – or, I should say, what the past held.

"Mr. Ryan," Dr. Hoitdle called out from behind the main controls of the many computers and flashing lights that were now in full flow. I turned to look at him. "Safe travels, I'll be seeing you soon, my boy," he said, like a father speaking to a son heading off on a voyage to see the world.

Without uttering a word, I just nodded once and turned to Sara. "Ladies first," I said, pointing to the entrance. She stepped through the doorway and I started to follow. I took one last look behind me and wondered if I'd ever see this place again, or any of my friends and family for that matter. I entered the belly of the beast.

As we got inside, the rest of the teams of white-coats and our thick-necked head of security, Hermann Leitman, started to load all of Sara and Eddie's photographic equipment into the dome. As the last piece of equipment was placed in with us, Leitman looked at me and without saying a word, just smirked and let out a false, contemptuous laugh, which sent a shiver down my spine, telling me he knew something I didn't. But here I was, still pushing through and going against everything my instincts were telling me, which was to get out and run. *Run as fast as you can, take Sara with you, and never look back.*

"Move it, bone-head, go buy yourself a neck," Eddie said to our not-so-friendly minder, as he stepped into the dome. I let a laugh slip out and as Sara smiled too, it suddenly released the tension that had been building up in the air. Leitman just looked pissed off and walked away muttering to himself.

"So, are we all packed for a trip back in time?" Eddie quipped.

"Sure, why not?" Sara quickly replied, looking at me.

"Let's do this," I added.

Eddie stood at the entrance and shouted out, "Okay, let's get this baby revved up, people!" and came back inside, giggling to himself.

The hydraulic doors started to make a grinding sound as they slowly came together in the middle.

"No escape now," Sara said. No one replied.

The dome started to hum; the bright lights started to glow. I gulped and waited in anticipation for what was coming. Sara took my hand once more and closed her eyes. Eddie nodded to me and stood in silence. *For once,* I thought.

As the power of the dome breathed life it started to create engine-like sounds gaining in strength. The lights were circling now with increasing intensity. It was hard to focus on any one thing. Sara's eyes were still closed. If this was to be my last moment alive, I wanted to see it happen. I kept my eyes open for as long as I could. The sound increased. The deafening sounds of the dome were almost too much to bear; Sara let go of my hand and covered her ears, and we all followed her lead and tried to block out the piercing sound of BETI's cries. Sara yelled out, "I can't take this!"

"Hold on, it won't be long," I yelled at the top of my voice. We started to fall to our knees and hold our heads in towards our chests, curling up into balls to try hiding from the pain, when suddenly one final deafening bang was the last thing we heard as we fell into darkness and unconsciousness.

"John! John, wake up, can you hear me?" I heard a muffled voice through my pained ears. "Is he alive?" I thought I recognized the voice. "Yes, of course he's alive," came the other voice again. I knew that voice. It was Sara. I slowly started to come around and as I tried to open my eyes, I felt the bright daylight shine into my eyes forcing me to squint. After a minute or two, I could start to see the blurred faces of Sara and Eddie kneeling over me.

"Hi," I said. The two of them fell back on their asses and laughed out loud.

"What a rush, eh?" Eddie beamed.

"I thought my head was going to explode," Sara replied.

I was flat on my back and sat up quick, felt a dizzy spell come over me and quickly asked, "What happened? Tell me we're alive, and this isn't heaven, or hell....I mean, are we here, did it work? Are we back in 1941?"

Eddie and Sara looked at each other, and Sara replied, "Yes, we believe we are." "But how can you be sure?" I asked again.

Eddie pointed over my shoulder and said, "What do you think that is?"

I turned and looked back; my eyes were still trying to focus, but to my astonishment, I could make out the recently burned-out and crashed remains of a German fighter plane, a Messerschmitt

109, the backbone of the Luftwaffe's fighter force. As my vision improved, I could also see the body of the pilot hanging through the cockpit, with his face covered in dried blood and bullet holes riddling his body.

"Okay," I said. "I guess that's pretty convincing."

"We've got to get a bearing on where we are exactly, and then start what we came here to do," Eddie said in an uncharacteristically steady, reasonable voice.

I carefully stood up and took in my surroundings. We were in a densely-wooded forest. I could feel the cool air, and looking at my 1930s-issued watch, I could see it was 10:32 a.m. The ground was damp, but it didn't look like it had rained the night before. Not much sunlight was getting through the cloudy sky and tightly packed trees that surrounded us, but I could see why we were transported here. It gave us the best chance of being hidden away from German troops or unfriendly locals.

Turning my eyes to the ground, I could see all our equipment had travelled safely too. Eddie had already opened some crates and began taking out his modern camera recording equipment, disguised inside 1940s outer coverings. Sara, too, had her photography equipment disguised to look like an old camera from the 1940s, looking just like a camera well-used from a few years of travel around the world.

One crate remained unbroken. It was, just like the others, unmarked. I knelt and popped open the lid with the use of a penknife Eddie had brought with him. I looked up at Sara and Eddie and said, "Well, I guess Hoitdle is taking no chances." I reached in and pulled out a German P08 Luger pistol and handed it to Eddie. "Nice," was all he said. I removed the other two, handed one to Sara and placed my own on the ground beside me. I took out the rounds of ammunition and handed them out. Each Luger was capable of taking eight rounds in each clip and one in the chamber; I knew the theory, but when it came to actually using one, I was a little unsure. Just as I started to fumble around with the loading, Sara grabbed the Luger off me and said, "Here, let me show you." Without hesitation, she loaded eight rounds into the clip, slamming it into the gun, pulling back the clip, and handing it back to me. "Oh, and don't forget about the safety," she said with a smile on her face.

"Thanks," I said, taking the Luger and looking it over on both sides. Eddie laughed and just said, "Wow, impressive."

The crate also contained three leather carry-bags with straps where we could place our three extra fully-loaded Luger clips, and our weapon. We also had our identity papers and our own equipment. For me, it was the plans which I was to reveal to Hitler – if I could actually manage to pull off the near-impossible feat of getting into his headquarters.

Eddie and Sara packed away their final pieces of film materials and stood there waiting for me to say something.

"Well, I guess this is it, time to say our goodbyes," I said, feeling anxious. Eddie just nodded. Sara took five steps over to me and said, "How about au revoir? Until we meet again." And with that, she kissed me on both cheeks and once on the mouth, then took a few steps back.

"Good luck, Ryan, see you on the other side," Eddie said kindly and turned to find his way out of the woods. Sara smiled once more at me and followed close behind Eddie. I watched them until they fell out of sight and I was left there alone. We both had different directions to head in. Mine was towards the East Prussian town of Rastenburg, which was eight kilometres from where Hitler was stationed at the *Wolfsschanze*, the Wolf's Lair. I opened out a map which was with my mission papers along with a compass and looked over the directions outlined for me in red. Once I found my bearings, I folded the map and placed it in my satchel, and the compass in my side pocket. Flinging the satchel over my shoulder, I buttoned up my grey woollen coat and set out to find the road to Rastenburg.

I made my way through the dense forest for about thirty minutes and eventually I could see a clearing up ahead. As I got to the edge of the clearing, I crouched down to survey what was ahead. I felt uneasy about stepping out into open ground, but I had no choice. Considering my location and the importance of who was located not too far away, I felt it was only a matter of time before I stumbled across a German patrol, or unfriendly locals in the area. Taking one more panoramic view and seeing nothing of immediate danger, I stood up, took a breath, ventured out into the clearing and headed towards what looked like fencing about half a mile to the north of the clearing. *Should come to a road*, I thought to myself, *according to the map*. To my left I spotted a few cows staring in my direction as I made my way forward; they soon went back to grazing on the grass. Ten minutes later, I arrived at the fence and on the other side was indeed the road I was looking for. I was to veer left and head west which to head to Rastenburg.

I looked right and then left and seeing no one around, I stepped up onto the fence and climbed over to reach the other side. Re-adjusting my leather satchel, I started out along the road. I worked out it should take me a further twenty-five minutes to reach the outskirts of the town, where I knew there would be German checkpoints and roaming patrols on every street and road in and out of Rastenburg. As I strolled along, my mind turned to Sara and Eddie; I wondered how they were doing. To be honest, my mind was really on Sara. I hoped she was safe. I already missed her, and wished she was with me now.

Eddie and Sara had their own plans. They had to make their way through as many occupied territories as possible, starting in Poland, then south to Czechoslovakia, and west through Austria and Slovenia and then meeting up back up in Paris before finally returning to Germany where we had to make contact with a young Doctor Hoitdle working on a non-functioning time machine, with me as the missing link.

The whole plan, I still thought, was absurd and most likely a suicide mission, but yet here I was walking along the road to Rastenburg in 1941, in the hope of offering victory plans to Adolf Hitler to ensure he won the war. "No problem," I sniggered to myself.

One of my many fears was if I succeeded in my plans, and Germany won the war, how was I then supposed to convince Hitler to release me, to allow me to make my way to Doctor Hoitdle? What if Hitler kept me prisoner with these new plans? I would be handing Germany the war with no way home, and find myself stuck in the foreign world of 1941 to live out my life under Nazi control. I envisaged Hitler honoring me in some way, a hero to their cause for helping them win the war. My family gone; history changed. Everything I knew, dead. A new world order and a different future. Only three people would know of the future we call the twenty-first century: myself, Eddie and Sara. I would be forced to live with the consequences of such an incredibly outlandish and dangerous plan, just to answer the timeless question, asked of every historian and World War Two enthusiast, "What if Hitler had won the war?"

Somehow, I just could not stop myself from striding on towards the unknown, and towards a destiny of unparalleled infamy.

Chapter 8
Capture

Coming to a sign that read *Rastenburg 1km*, I knew I had arrived on the edge of the town. I tucked myself into the side of the road, where some heavy bushes helped cover me. I peered over the top, and coming into my view about two hundred meters away, I could see a vehicle that looked like a jeep parked back into a slight opening between some tall trees. I could see no movement at this time. But then, suddenly, to my rear I could hear the sound of vehicles coming from about half a mile away. I jumped deep into the bushes and landed down a sloped wet ditch to hide out of sight, waiting to see what was coming. The sound got nearer and as they approached, they roared past and I could see three vehicles. Two transport military trucks, a Krupp L3H163 with what looked like about ten SS troops in each, and, leading at the front, a Nazi S.d.Kfz. 251 half-track, with a mounted machine gun and another six soldiers on board.

I waited for them to pass. They arrived at the position of that jeep I spotted, and four guards appeared out into the middle of the road and stopped the convoy to check for papers. I guessed this was a first checkpoint, one of many I could not yet fully see from my position. One guard circled the first vehicle, the half-track, looking inside while another guard checked the undercarriage. They were eventually waved through and I watched them move on and out of sight around a tree-lined bend.

I had to decide now. Did I just waltz on up to the checkpoint, make myself known to the guards and demand to see a senior officer, or try to make my way into the town and hand myself in to the local Gestapo police, in the hope that they would take me seriously enough to listen to an Irishman wandering around East Prussia? Of course, at first, I would be asking to meet with the local military commander of the town, with my initial cover of looking to obtain weapons for the IRA. But once in, I would have to reveal my real intention. After careful consideration, I thought I would have a better chance with the SS guards if I could just get them to pass along the information to their commander, and hope that from there it would be in turn passed to one of the senior officers stationed at the Wolf's Lair. It was slim, but better than the alternative. I feared if I was in the hands of the Gestapo, they would see me as a spy and torture me into revealing what they believed I was here for; not something I wanted to find out. I could be handed over to them by the SS guards, but it was a risk I needed to take. I believed if I could convince them I had vital information about plans of an imminent attack on their Führer, then they might, just might, get to someone high up in the ranks where Hitler was stationed. I had to ensure that I got inside, where I knew I had a chance of convincing Hitler, as he was one of a select few people aware of a weapon currently being secretly tested by his team of scientists. He would surely at the very least want to know how I had this information, and demand to see me or have me questioned by Goebbels. At least, that was my plan – in fact, my only plan. It had to work, or I was a dead man for sure; or worse, left to the Gestapo to work on me for days or weeks, before shooting me in the back of the head and left in a ditch to rot, another forgotten, unknown civilian casualty of the war. My only consolation would be that at least Hitler would never know of our plans and would still end up losing the war if I was tossed aside as a demented madman. That would be the only redemption to this fantastical plan.

And so, I got up and walked into the middle of the road and started making my way towards the checkpoint. As I got closer around the bend, I could see movement now and a checkpoint hut, with heaving mounted machine guns sprouting out from built-up walls of sandbags. I could see the guards' heads turning to stare out towards me. To the left of the checkpoint, in a small clearing was a Panzer III with its 37mm gun pointing down the road in my direction.

As I got closer, two SS guards stepped out in front of the checkpoint with their machine guns pointed at me and started shouting in German, "*Halt, halt.*" Indeed, I did halt, and held my hands up to show I was not a threat. "*Komm her,*" shouted one of the SS guards, and from my very limited German, I knew he meant 'come here.' "*Papiere, papiere,*" he yelled at me. I slowly pointed at my satchel to show them I was reaching for my papers, and then I remembered my Luger. *Damn it,* I thought, *should have tossed it earlier.* Too late now. I didn't want them to assume I stole it or took it from a German officer and was fearful of what they would think. I took my bag off and placed it on the ground and reached in for my identity papers then held them up while placing my bag on the ground. One of the guards waved his fingers inwards towards me indicating to give them to him. I reached out and he lowered his machine gun to take them while the other guard held his weapon pointed at me with a finger on the trigger. I looked past the two guards; the other guards at the checkpoint seemed unfazed by the new arrival. I guess they stopped and checked many convoys, and saw visitors pass through all day.

The guard looked at my Patrick O'Reilly papers intently and then looked me up and down. He held his gaze on my face for a few moments before asking me what I wanted here. I had to be honest and say I could not speak German and needed to speak to someone who did. "Irish," I said. He looked at me, puzzled, and said something to the other guard, who just shrugged his shoulders. The guard handed me back my papers and using his gun he ushered me towards the checkpoint. I picked up my bag, threw it over my shoulder and walked towards the other guards while one of them remained standing, looking out in the direction I came from almost as if instinct was telling him never to trust anyone and to ensure I was alone. I got to the checkpoint and the barrier that blocked the road was lifted. I strolled through and stopped for directions as to what to do next. The SS guard who had checked my papers went inside the hut and picked up the telephone and waited for an answer. As I stood outside looking around, one of the guards pulled out a box of cigarettes and walked over to me.

"*Zigarette?*" he offered to me.

"Ah, no," I said in English, before quickly correcting myself. "*Nein, nein, danke.*" He took one out for himself, lit it, nodded once to me and re-took his position at the barrier.

The guard on the telephone talked down the line in German, all the while staring out at me, and I assumed he was trying to get someone in the town who could speak English to try find out what I wanted here. *A spy surely wouldn't just walk up to a German checkpoint*, I thought to myself, and hoped they would think the same.

The guard eventually hung up the telephone and came outside.

"*Warten Sie hier,*" I was ordered: I had to wait by the hut. I put my back up against its wooden walls and let myself slide down; I was feeling a little foot-sore from walking through the woods. All the guards went back to their positions and for the next two hours I was left waiting for, I presumed, whoever the guard had called to come out and get me. During those two hours, four different patrols and supply trucks had come and gone through without any fuss. I was hungry now and getting agitated. I tried to stay alert and not look like I was in the wrong place at the wrong time but that I was here with good reason.

Just as I was starting to feel myself drift off, I heard another vehicle approach from where I had wandered in. As it pulled up, I got back up onto my feet. The car stopped alongside me, and I saw the uniform. It was an SS Major, a Sturmbannführer in a

German staff car, a Horch 853, with a driver and one guard in the rear beside the Major.

The barrier was immediately raised and the car drove through and stopped to confront the guard who had read my papers.

After a brief talk with the guard, and a few glances in my direction, the Major summoned me over. He spoke in English.

"Your name is Patrick O'Reilly, Irish?" he inquired.

"Yes," I replied.

"What do you want here Irishman? You are a long way from home."

"Yes, Major; it's imperative I speak with someone from your staff headquarters," I informed him.

He understood what I was asking; he looked at me, surprised, and retorted immediately, "Why would you want to speak with them? And what would make you think you would be permitted to?"

I replied, "Major, this may not be the best place to discuss what I have to say, but I have vital information that needs to reach the highest possible ranks inside your headquarters. And by the highest, I mean *the* very highest." He looked me up and down, while rubbing his chin in thought.

"You had better come with me, get in." He ordered me into the front passenger seat where I could be watched. He sat down and shouted at the driver to move along in his strong, commanding German accent. As we drove along the road, there were more and more guards and heavier gun positions the nearer we approached to the town. We quickly arrived and drove through an open checkpoint as the guards already knew the Major's car and let him pass without delay.

The car drove through the streets and arrived outside what I assumed was the Major's quarters. The guard in the rear ordered me out and the Major marched in front of me into a stone-walled building. The guard nodded for me to follow. I walked inside where I saw two more guards and another SS soldier manning a large radio station. He hardly took notice of me and the Major turned and told me to sit down on the opposite side of the large, rustic desk. He ordered his two SS guards out and told them to shut the door behind them. All that remained was the Major, the radio controller and me.

"I am Major Ludwig Kepplinger of the Waffen SS."

I gulped, as the Waffen SS was the armed wing of the Nazi Party's SS organisation. They were considered the best of the best and had a reputation for brutality and dogged fighting skills. They were battle-hardened and extremely loyal to Hitler. You had to be of pure Aryan blood to get a command or serve in the Waffen SS. Major Kepplinger wore one of the highest medals on his uniform: the Knight's Cross of the Iron Cross. The man in front of me was someone to be feared and respected. He was about five feet eleven, and of medium build. He was handsome, and I guessed he was in his late thirties. He was clearly a man of authority and he wore it well. He took off his hat, revealing tightly-cut blond hair, and placed it on the desk in front of him. He sat down opposite me and without speaking, he pulled open a drawer to his right and took out a bottle of Polish vodka, a Soplica marked as 40% pure. He took out two small thick glasses and without asking if I wanted one, poured them both and placed the bottle on the table. He slid one glass over to my side and raised it to me and waited for me to take it. I wasn't a fan of vodka, but without hesitation, I picked up the glass and raised it towards the Major and we both knocked it back in one, each of us grimacing as the kick set in at the back of our throats. Whereas mine was in distaste, I could see his was in appreciation; I hoped I'd hidden it well.

"So, Irishman, down to business. Please tell me exactly what information you want to share with our senior command."

"Major, I have information in this satchel that I know will help Germany win this war, but how I know, and how I have this information in my possession, is going to be a little harder to explain," I replied.

"Please, continue," he said.

I remembered the Luger in my satchel and did not want to get caught hiding it, so decided the best course of action was to hand it over willingly now rather than trying to conceal it.

"One thing I must confess, Major, before I go any further, to show you that I mean no harm here. I have in my possession here a Luger, and I want to hand it over to you. I do not want to end up getting shot, so I'm surrendering you my bag and you can remove it yourself," I said calmly.

He raised his eyebrows and slowly leaned forward. I took the bag off my shoulder and slid it across the table. He pulled the satchel in, paused to look at me and then opened the bag. He reached in and removed the gun and the three clips giving me an expression of surprise that I had such a weapon in my possession. He opened a drawer on the left and placed it along with the clips inside. He took a look inside the bag and pulled out the remaining items. Maps, information on battle plans that had still yet to happen, and letters from Doctor Hoitdle to his younger self explaining how all this had come together.

I also had the initial dummy plans to buy weapons for the IRA.

"What is all this?" he asked.

I explained to him that the weapons purchase was not real, and that in fact I was here for something much more significant. I also told him my real name was John Ryan.

"Those there, Major, are the battle outcomes of every major German defeat between 1941 and 1944; but they also show the blueprints of how they can be reversed, and turned to victory," I replied.

He leaned back into his chair and scratched his forehead for a few moments and then burst into laughter.

"You almost had me there, Irishman." He was still laughing to himself. "Plans for 1944, interesting, plans to the future, I like it," he said in a patronising way.

I sat forward and said, "Major, you need to listen to me. These plans are for your Führer, and him alone. If you do not get me and these plans to him, you will regret this for the rest of your short life." Now the Major wasn't smiling anymore.

"Don't you play games with me, Ryan, or I will have you shot for spreading defeatism of the Fatherland," he yelled.

"Major, please understand I am not here to spread defeatism, the exact opposite in fact. I am here to help you win this war. I am here to bring final victory for the Third Reich," I retorted.

The Major stood up and walked over to the door.

I felt I was losing him. "All I ask is that you bring those papers to your Führer. There is information that only he will understand, and I promise you, he will be most pleased with you. Look, if I'm a mad man, then he will order me shot anyway, so what have you got to lose?" I said.

"Ha, only my dignity, my rank and maybe my head," he blurted back.

"But imagine your rewards if I'm right – the recognition from High Command," I said, trying to appeal to his ego.

He stood silent and walked around the room for a few more moments.

The radio operator appeared to take no notice as he had his headphones on covering his ears.

"I heard you Irish like a tall tale, but this, how is it even possible? Tell me that, Ryan," the Major asked.

"German ingenuity, Major. You cannot see it now, but in trying to create your superweapons, you developed a time machine that worked once during the war as a test and then many years from now it will be eventually brought to life for this very moment. I don't expect you to understand or believe me now, but if you just get this information to Goebbels or Hitler, I promise you this: you will be astoundingly rewarded," I informed him.

He walked back to his desk and lifted up some of the battle plans and shuffled them around trying to make some sense of it all. He placed them back on the desk and stood in silence for a few moments.

He once again marched to the door.

"Wait here," Major Kepplinger ordered, and he opened the door and went outside. One of his guards was ordered inside and stood guard at the open door watching me intensely. All the while the radio controller, still with his headphones on, continued about his business, spinning dials and taking down and writing out messages received.

Twenty minutes had passed when the Major eventually returned.

"Okay, Ryan, it looks like you've earned yourself a little more time. Come with me," he ordered me . I got up and grabbed all the papers and instructions from the desk and placed them back into the satchel and closed it over. I followed the Major outside and into his car once more. This time he told me to sit in the back with him. Only the driver was in the front, and we took off.

We headed east out of town and drove along a winding wooded road with ditches on either side. We passed more heavily-guarded checkpoints and roadside gun positions. The further we went, the more heavily guarded the positions seemed to get. We were heading eight kilometres east, deeper into the Masurian woods.

I knew where the Major was taking me. I presumed if I was to be shot it would have happened by now, and not by a highly decorated officer of the Waffen SS.

Twenty minutes later, we pulled up to a major checkpoint with at least thirty guards on positions high and low. Just past the checkpoint there was tall metal fencing covered with barbed wire and protected by high tower positions on both sides of a large double-gated entrance. The guards here were much sterner and ordered my satchel off. The Major just said, "Better give it to them."

Without questioning it, I removed the satchel and handed it over. It was handed over to another guard who stood back while another guard went through the items intently, mainly looking for explosives and weapons of any kind. After looking at me and the Major, the guard placed everything back in the satchel and hung onto it. They ordered me out of the car and began searching me thoroughly and not in a friendly manner. They pushed me back and nodded for me to get back into the car, which I did promptly. The guards ordered us through the checkpoint, and we drove right up to the gates. We waited for a moment as the machine gun tower guards pointed their heavy weapons in our direction. An SS officer walked out from a hut inside the fence and stood and looked at each one of us in turn.

It was getting dark now and as the light was fading, the officer pulled out a torch he had in his side belt and shone it in my face first and then the driver and finally the Major who did not object. This was one checkpoint that the Major was not going to be waved on through with impunity.

After a few more moments the officer stood back and ordered the guards inside to open the gates. Four guards with machine guns flung over their shoulders raced forward from a position further back to approach the gates. They split into groups of two and pulled open the chain around the gates and took off a heavy wooden barrier running across on the inside. They all pulled the gates inwards and once they were fully opened, the officer with the torch signalled to us to enter. We drove on through and were met by more guards who ordered the driver to pull the car over to the right and down a side driveway where four more guards ordered us to halt.

One of the guards came around to where the Major was sitting and asked for his identity papers, which the Major took out and handed over to the guard without hesitation. The guard took one look at the Major and handed him back his papers.

"Get out, Ryan," the Major ordered. The guards directed me inside a side entrance into a concrete structure, about a hundred yards from the main complex that I could see over to the right of the gated entrance.

I did not delay and went inside where two more guards met me inside. The Major followed.

"You must wait here, Ryan, until further instructions," the Major said.

"Okay, Major," was all I could muster. This was not a place you asked questions.

"Just through there, you will find food and water. I'm sure you are hungry after your journey."

"Yes, thank you, Major, I am," I replied thankfully.

"Good. I will be back as soon as I can, so please cooperate with these men," he said to me, meaning well.

I just nodded, and he turned and left.

The guards ushered me inside to the next room, again fully protected with heavy reinforced concrete and there indeed in front of me on a long wooden table was a mixture of fruits, cold meats, some small pastries and jugs of water. The guards closed the heavy steel doors behind them, and I heard it lock. I walked to the table and surveyed the goodies in front of me. I dug in and started with the meats. The thick cuts tasted fresh, and stronger in flavour than I was used to. I poured some water into one of the glasses on the table and drank back three glasses of water to quench my thirst. I ate some more meat to fill my belly before moving onto an apple. I sat down on the bench in front of the table and gazed back towards the door, looking around the room and I noticed wiring in the top corner. Perhaps it was bugged, or wiring for a telephone, or maybe wired for explosives.

I assumed bugging would be the most likely.

The room was cold and smelled musty, but it was dry. The stone walls were covered over by poured concrete. The paint was coming off the walls, and the ceiling had only one light hanging from the centre. There was a lone picture of Adolf Hitler hanging to the right side of the room and nothing else.

I couldn't help wondering what this room was really used for, even though I had never read about any rooms being used for anything relating to torture in the Wolf's Lair.

An hour went by and I was getting numb in my butt muscles, so got up to walk around. Just then I heard the steel door start to open and in walked two SS guards.

"*Aus, aus,*" they shouted. I knew they meant 'out, out', and I quickly went out of the room and into the hallway. They pushed me back to the first room I had come through, and there was a face I was very familiar with: Paul Joseph Goebbels, Reich Minister of Propaganda of Nazi Germany, and Hitler's second-in-command and most loyal follower. His face was just as I had seen in old black-and-white photographs in history books, sunken and pointed. He was not a handsome man; stern and cold. His eyes seemed lifeless, and he had a smirk on his face as I arrived and stood in front of him. Two guards stood either side of him and ordered me to halt. Just then, Major Kepperlinger came back in and stood to the Reich Minister's left and introduced Goebbels to me. "I am here to translate what you have to say to the Minister," the Major said.

And so, I once more began my tall tale of my mission and how I came to be here in 1941 German-controlled Prussia.

The whole time, I was not interrupted once by the Minister. His expressionless face never changed. From time to time, I would look at the Major and see him go through various pained expressions.

When I was finally through, the Minister just looked at the Major and waved him away to the side.

Goebbels walked to me and stared into my eyes while the two guards either side of him stayed close by, pointing their machine guns right at my body.

"*Der Führer wird dich jetzt sehen,*" he said sternly, and turned and walked out. Both guards followed him.

When they left the Major spoke. "Well, Ryan, it looks like you will be seeing the Führer after all." He sounded surprised.

I just looked up and took a breath and said, "Are you sure, Major?"

He replied, "It looks like the Führer has seen your plans and is very interested in the information you have brought him. It appears he wants to find out whether indeed you are telling the truth or not. But be careful, Ryan. Our Führer is not a patient man. If he feels you are lying, you will be shot immediately. So please, tread carefully." He spoke as if he were warning an old friend. I just nodded my head a few times and began to think of how I would begin my crazy story, how I would introduce myself and how I would feel standing in front of the most feared man of the twentieth century.

Chapter 9
Convincing Hitler

Two SS guards brought me to the entrance of the main complex. I recognised the reinforced concrete structure from the ruins that we see on documentaries today. They banged on the steel doors, which opened a few moments later. I was pushed inside, and the doors closed firmly behind me. We marched down a short corridor and came to steps that curved around and down to the right.

I counted out twenty-five steps – for what reason, I had no idea. Maybe to try and keep my mind focused. At each section and turn were more guards. Staff both male and female were carrying on with their normal duties, and they all seemed disinterested in me. We followed on through more corridors and down another set of steps till we hit what I believed to be the very bottom level. The guards brought me past a kitchen and into the next room which had storage lockers in them and told me to wait. They stood guard at the doors; I waited.

What felt like an eternity, but was only twenty minutes, later, I heard a large door open and orders being quietly given out. The two SS guards called me out into the corridor and searched me one more time. They ushered me forward and one of the guards opened the large steel door in front of us and went inside. He came back out and ordered me though. The other guard followed behind.

And as I ventured through into the dimly lit room. there sitting down behind his map-filled desk was the man I had been sent here to meet. The Führer himself: Adolf Hitler. I didn't even notice the small stout man standing to my right side, who began to speak. "Mr. John Ryan, I am pleased to introduce the Führer. I am Ernst Bachmann, and I will be the interpreter for this meeting, if it pleases you," he said.

"Yes, of course, and thank you," I replied, and followed up with, "And thank *you*, Führer, for agreeing to see me in these most unusual circumstances." Bachmann relayed my words.

Hitler just sat there for a while, firing his steely eyes at me. He stood up, came around his large desk and stared into my eyes, as if trying to see right into my soul.

He looked at his guards and ordered them out. They looked at each other and with a slight pause yelled out, "*Heil* Hitler," and left, closing the door behind them.

"*Nein, Nein, Nein.* I will have you taken out and shot, if one more word comes out of your treacherous mouth."

"I am not lying, and if you do not listen to what I have to say you will be remembered in history as the most hated, vile and evil leader that ever existed. This, I can assure you," I was shouting at Hitler. "You will lose this war, and you will lose it disastrously. I can help you win and change your destiny. The way it should have been." I could hardly believe the words coming from my own mouth. The interpreter waited for the next words to come out of Hitler's mouth.

Rounding his large paper-filled wooden desk, Hitler approached and stood two feet away from me, and turned his head up to meet mine. His cold eyes buried deep into mine and he held my gaze for what felt like an eternity.

Without speaking a word, the man in front of me raised his hand and waited for me to grasp it. In near-disbelief I looked at his pale hand and gave him my shaking hand in return. With three shakes he let it go.

He smiled at me, said nothing, turned and walked slowly back behind his desk. He looked down at a large map laid out, pushing aside some papers, and smiled.

Hitler had been aware for some time that he had had his secret team of scientists, made to work around the clock to amass powerful weapons for the Third Reich. One of those powerful weapons had produced a result that astounded and surpassed even Hitler's expectations. He was aware that some type of powerful magnetic pulse was about to help turn the tide of war in his favour if it could work on the battlefield. To everyone's amazement, they had discovered what this incredible new technology was capable of, and he demanded the full weight of the régime's support be given to ensuring success of this weapon.

Of course, at this time it was still at early testing stages, and my grandfather, well aware of how dangerous this machine was, had already created his failsafe security, but the Nazis were none the wiser at this time. Hitler, unaware of this, continued with his battle plans across Europe and waited for news to ensure Germany of the absolute victory he demanded.

Once I had informed Hitler of my awareness of this machine, and of the two senior protagonists working together to make this happen, Hitler realised that I could be in fact telling the truth. The two names I gave were Doctor Ralf Hoitdle and my grandfather, Joseph John Ryan. Maybe, just maybe, he started to believe that if in fact Doctor Hoitdle and my grandfather had got it working so that time travel did exist, then the destiny of Germany and the Third Reich was now firmly in his dictatorial hands.

Here I was, four years before Hitler was supposed to take his own life—when he would inform a chosen few, including Doctor Hoitdle so they could find a way to re-ignite the fires of Europe by finding a solution to their impotent weapon—standing in the midst of evil trying to convince Adolf Hitler that it was he himself who had made this happen right before his death, four years from now. That giving his last order in that rank filled bunker had now brought us to this point, back from the future with plans and information that would empower Hitler and show him the path to glory for all Germany.

He turned away from me and walked back to the other side of his desk and panned his eyes on that large map of Europe on his desk.

He lifted his head and still smiling, he nodded his head up and down a few times, he said, "*Nun, Meister Ryan, es scheint, das Schicksal aller Deutschland ist jetzt in deinen Händen. Zeig mir den Weg zum Sieg.*"

I looked at the interpreter and heard his words: "Well, Mr. Ryan, it appears the fate of all Germany is now in your hands. Show me the way to victory."

With that, I asked for my satchel. Bachmann walked to the door, opened it and ordered the guards to bring it at once.

Hitler and I stood there staring at each other and did not take our eyes off the other the whole time.

He was testing my resolve.

Just as I felt the gulping in my throat would show too much fear, the knock on the door broke the tension.

The stout man opened the door and took the bag and handed it to me.

I opened it and took out a twenty-page document, with detailed information of five major battles. Five main mistakes that historians and other leading military leaders have debated for years, where they believe Germany could have won the war from 1941.

The document was titled the *Five Plan Solution*. And here I was, about to divulge this audacious plan to Adolf Hitler.

Chapter 10
The Five Plan Solution

THE PLAN WAS BROKEN DOWN into five major mistakes Hitler made during the war.

The first: not killing off the RAF and underestimating British radar which could pick up German fighters and bombers coming across the English Channel allowing their own fighters to intercept them.

The second: attacking Russia before finishing off the threat of the Allies in the West, and to what Churchill called the weak underbelly of the Nazis, namely Italy, Sicily and Malta.

The third: allowing English codebreakers to figure out German coded communications with the Enigma machine, which allowed them to know all of Germany's future battle plans and top-secret movements.

The fourth: once ready to attack Russia, doing it in Blitzkrieg movements rather than in force. Russia was too vast, so where this tactic might have worked against an over-whelmed and under-prepared French-Anglo army, it could not work in Mother Russia. Supply lines would be too stretched. Oil would run short, slowing or halting the movement of truck supplies, panzer divisions and the Luftwaffe Airforce. Then the winter weather would set in, and an unprepared German army would get bogged down and freeze in arctic conditions they were just not prepared for. They needed the right winter clothing, equipment that did not jam in freezing weather, and uninterrupted supply lines to the front and a much larger military force of manpower, tanks, supplies, ammunition and the airforce for a steady but forceful attack on the Red Army. Taking the Crimea would protect the flank for a major offensive attack on Moscow. Stalingrad, which proved a disastrous torn in Hitler's side, was to be side-stepped. If Moscow fell, Russia would fall with it.

The fifth: Moscow itself. Attack from all sides with the full force of the German Wehrmacht. It must fall. With Europe, Normandy, the Baltics and Africa sown up, this would allow Germany to pull on the full resources of the German Empire.

If Moscow fell and the Swastika was flying over Red Square, the will of the people and its moral would surely deteriorate, and the rest of Russia should fall. And if it fell it would once again allow the German army to consolidate, to bring the supply lines closer, airfields, tank factories, supplies and oil reserves, and to finally finish off the rest of the Red Army, which at that stage would be in vast retreat and unable to supply itself.

You cannot fight a war on two major fronts.

Finish the objectives in the West and the Baltics, including North Africa and then bring the full force of the German armed forces to bear on Russia.

And there it was: a strategy that as much as it seemed possible was still a long way off being achieved. And there was one more issue that was looming further into the future of 1945; the United States of America had developed the atom bomb. The war would have to be won within two years, or it would not only be Japan that would suffer from the might of the American war machine. If Germany could win the war by 1943, they too could start to develop their own weapons programme with the vast wealth of conquered countries and all the resources that come with that from, money, gold, minerals, oil, iron ore, millions and millions in slave labour and the top scientists from all of Europe and Germany combined. The possibilities were endless.

As plans got underway almost immediately, Hitler had recalled his generals to his war room to start a bombing campaign on the radar stations across the United Kingdom. He demanded this be done within the next four days, and then to follow on with a massive air assault on their airfields. He pulled as much of his Luftwaffe airforce as possible to attack British fighters and bring England to its knees. This would leave German U-Boats and naval battleships to control the seas and block all British-bound supplies, effectively isolating the United Kingdom.

Along with this new plan, he put a halt on the attack on Russia until these first three objectives were concluded, which, he was informed by his generals, could be completed within the next four to five weeks.

With the United Kingdom crippled and Churchill isolated he would be free to turn his attention to the Baltics and ensure that Italy was re-enforced even further. He doubled Italian and German troops there and sent heavier bombing raids to Malta. UK naval supplies were not able to support Malta, as they were forced to withdraw any available assets to protect them from total annihilation. German and Italian forces were able to move in and wrap up that soft under-belly and turn it into a stronghold, just like fortress Europe.

As the days turned into weeks, I was embedded in with Hitler and his crazy faithful followers who seemed to be in a haze of battle-frenzied victorious delirium as one battle win turned into another and another until the weeks turned into months, and before long we saw the map of Europe turn red and black with Swastika flags swarming all over Europe, from the edges of Western France to the lower regions of the Baltics and North Africa, to the very borders of Russia until Germany secured all its initial plans to take all of Europe, Scandinavia, North Africa and the Baltics, only leaving one final battle: the vast regions of Russia, the mother of all battles. This time, Germany would be able to attack with a force of unforeseen magnitude, a rejuvenated army with three times the men available, rested, fed and high on the countless victories that seemed never to end. An army that was supported with the right supply lines and warm winter clothing; weapons that would not jam in freezing weather; hundreds of thousands of anti-tank portable cannons; and a mass-produced airforce along with an armada of twenty-five thousand tanks, the like of which has never been seen before and will most likely be never seen again.

The world held its breath.

Chapter 11
Russia's Fall

WHILE GERMANY WAS BATHING IN an avalanche of blood-drenched, one-sided, relentless victory after victory and rolling towards the vast but now vulnerable eastern front, my mind often drifted to other places and other people. I often thought of my family and home. I thought of Sara and Eddie and wondered if they were still alive or captured as spies. But if I am honest, it was Sara that invaded my mind the most – where she was now, what she had seen, and whether she had captured the pictures she and Eddie had dreamt of. Was she okay, and did she think of me? I had missed her, her soft face and her direct manner. I looked forward to seeing her once again. I hoped I would one day hold her hand and get the chance to kiss her full rosy lips and share our own experiences of what the world was now witnessing.

I was held here now, at the Wolf's Lair, the prized possession of the fast-growing Nazi empire, guiding the war this way and that. Hitler had given me the highest protection. His elite SS guards were never to leave my side. He kept me close like his little puppet, but it was me who was pulling the strings for now; strings I wanted to cut every day, but I knew I had to play out this terrible new history to its ultimate conclusion. So, as the world held its breath and Russia awaited its pending fate, the vast German Wehrmacht moved its armies, airforce and armoured divisions into key attack positions, just like a chess player moving pieces into positions on a chess board. Very soon, it would be check-mate.

Before my military interventions on the 22nd of June 1941 had turned the tide of the war, in our original time and history during the start of Operation Barbarossa Germany had at their disposal 3,795 tanks, 4,000 fighter jets, 1,500 bombers, 20,000 artillery pieces, 17,000 mortars, 600 armoured vehicles and 3.8 million men. But now, since I virtually handed Hitler the war on a silver plate with a total victory in Europe, the Baltics, Scandinavia, and North Africa, they could pull the full forces of their military might down to bear on Russian territories. With my treacherous information, Hitler had amassed a superior force of 25,000 tanks, 12,000 fighters, 3,500 bombers, 60,000 artillery pieces, 45,000 mortars, 2,800 armoured vehicles moving more supplies and support materials along with fuel and a massive eight million soldiers made up of victorious Axis powers, with troops from Romania, Italy, Hungary, Austria, Slovakia, Croatia, Bulgaria, Yugoslavia and pro-Nazi Finnish soldiers, all led by the battle-hardened German Wehrmacht and SS divisions. That was without mentioning the many puppet states under Hitler's influence, all of which Germany could pull vast resources from, along with millions and millions of both forced and unforced labour building the Nazis all the military power and might they need twenty-four hours a day, seven days a week, round the clock. It was non-stop production of weapons of war, to crush their hated Slavic enemy in the East. Their soldiers were now well-supplied with ammunition, winter clothing, fuel for tanks and aircraft and armoured vehicles. Battle victories would come quicker than before and avoiding getting bogged in the mud filled roads and fields of Russia and before the winter set in to halt the oncoming Nazi tsunami.

There was no stopping them now, it seemed.

To my horror, my hands ran red with the blood of millions of lives and of many more to come. I had to force myself every minute to try believing this was not real. It would be back to the way it was when my life was all about graduating college and drinking beer. It all seemed so trivial now. But yet I missed it. I missed my family; I missed my loud-mouthed buddy, Paul Duffy. I missed my apartment, and my walks to the bus. But most of all, I missed Sara and I missed my life. I wish I could go back and take Sara with me and forget this whole hideous plan. Alas, I knew the only way of getting home now was completing our mission to the very bitter end.

As Germany made its final preparations in its build-up on the borders of Russia, it was now February 1942, a year later than our history books had told us, as Germany now ensured this time the offensive would be at the right moment with superior numbers and, of course, the knowledge that I had divulged in our plans to hand the Nazis world domination. I was able to convince Hitler to pause rather than rushing into Russia in 1941. He now realized the importance of nullifying England and the Allied forces all over Europe and Scandinavia and shoring up Norway's coastline. He was aware that with America's industrial power and military might, he could not afford an American invasion leading to the ultimate downfall of a war on two fronts. So securing the Western borders with greater numbers was part of the German plans to ensure that if an invasion by the Allies ever came, it would be a damning risk which would cost them dearly.

I waited, and the world waited with me. It began as the first German planes flew across the Russian borders to begin a steadier and more controlled blitzkrieg than normal, and the final decisive battle against Hitler's main goal rolled into action. The sheer number of tiger tanks rolling towards town after town had the Russians retreating before they had a chance to engage. This time, Hitler would not divide his armies. There would be no army group North, South or Centre. There would be one massive swarm of armour and men pouring into cities to crush the enemy with no chance of a counterattack from the Russians. As cities fell, soldiers from Germany's allies, Romania and Bulgaria, would remain to act as security forces to ensure scattered Russian forces could not regroup and mount flanking attacks. It was not long before Germany's first armoured divisions arrived on the outskirts of Moscow.

It was thought that if Moscow fell, then Stalin would flee, and Russia would surrender. Germany remained outside Moscow until its full forces had caught up and formed a horseshoe armed guard around the city.

Stalin knew he was at the brink, and was told by his leading generals to flee the country.

In one massive attack, Germany unleashed a reign of hell down on Moscow, with round-the-clock shelling, tank bombardments and Luftwaffe air attacks, and within two days the city lay in ruins and most of the soldiers defending the city had died or fled. As the foot soldiers and tanks moved in, the city was in shell-shock and there was nowhere to hide. The Kremlin was in tatters and there was little sign of resistance.

Stalin had indeed fled in a Russian bomber and barely escaped to England via Greenland. He demanded the people of Russia rise up and defend the Motherland, but alas with no food and supplies, the people of Russia had no stomach to resist the power of this mighty Nazi force. Most of the surrounding cities with Russian commands like Rostokino, Lublino, Sviblovo and Veshnyaki had laid down their arms and either fled into hiding or surrendered in the fleeting hope of being fed by the Germans. Alas, this would be their final mistake.

German forces once again regrouped and left large occupying forces, this time made up of both German and Axis powers to ensure Hitler's prized asset would not fall back into Russian hands. They then turned east and headed for Stalingrad. This time there would be no long drawn out winter battlefield and years of hell for the Germans. With millions of Russian forces and armoured divisions captured or dead and airfields in the hands of the Luftwaffe, Russia was left with no leader, no plan, no air support to fight or drop supplies, and with hunger on the rise along with little ammunition, Russian commanders had a choice to surrender Stalingrad now along with the rest of its vast country to keep it from being totally destroyed just like Moscow. There was no fight left in them. It was futile to fight to the death in the hope of England and the United States somehow managing to mount an invasion. With time running out, and against Stalin's wishes, the Russians offered to surrender to German forces if they would offer medical and food supplies to its citizens and their ragged war-torn forces. The Germans, looking to finish off the war early, agreed, and an armistice was signed. Russia was now under full and total control by Germany and Hitler. Stalin, feeling betrayed in his secret hideaway in the countryside of western England, retreated into a lonely solace and contemplated suicide.

Germany now held the oil-rich fields of the Ukraine along with its iron ore, coal and natural gas; and, of course, its highly-productive wheat and corn fields. It was fair to say that Germany now controlled all the resources of Europe and could ensure its continued military might, supply lines and security. For the hundreds of millions of people that now answered to Germany, trying to rise up or speak out against the Third Reich would be like biting the hand that fed them. Berlin celebrated as the rest of the world looked on in horror. Perhaps this is what the Roman empire probably looked like to many; this was the new world order, and it was Nazi.

With the war in the East and West over, it was now time for Germany to decide what to do with its new-found territorial gains and wealth. With no one stumbling across the many death camps of the Jews and other political prisoners, Germany would not pay for its crimes against humanity. The victors write the history books, and so it would come to pass. On 30th September 1942, there would be no VE day, but instead what the Germans call, SFH Day: *Sieg Für Hitler* Day or 'Victory for Hitler' Day.

As the whole of Germany drank themselves into oblivion on the highs of victory and hailed their Führer Adolf Hitler, I turned my attentions to getting out of the clutches of the SS, to try find Sara and Eddie, so we could gather our damning evidence and get the hell back to our own time. This was becoming a tough task as Hitler treated me as some sort of messiah, wanting me close by all the time. I had to come up with a plan to get away.

I needed to gain his utmost trust and try to manipulate him to lower his guard. And so, I decided to try persuading him to allow me to travel across Europe, so I could document the Third Reich, to give the people of Germany my vision from an outsider's point of view; to show the world how great the German people really were and to show their acts of mercy, even though this was against everything the Nazis stood for. But the German High Command knew that they had to allow the world inside their empire at some stage. They could not insulate themselves to the whole world. Time would move on, and they wanted the rest of the world to look at them in admiration and not only fear. Hitler had gained the living space he had so sought after, he had rid Europe of communism, and most importantly Germany had come up with a solution to the Jewish question. And it was a question he did not want anyone outside of his Nazi state finding out about. I felt I had proved my loyalty in helping Germany win the war and now it was time for me to show the world the greatness and mercy of the Germany people through the eyes of an Irishman who was close to Hitler and could tell the people of the world that Germany was in fact no different to any other empire from history.

After much convincing, Hitler came around and was intrigued by my ideas. He thought if I could sell this by putting together a manifesto that I could present to the rest of the world, mainly England, the United States and its allies, then maybe it would prevent an attack by them in the future. If they could reach out and offer a peace pact, then that would help secure against any further aggression, even though Hitler now believed that no one could touch his vast empire. He felt invincible, and knew that anyone trying to bring down his Third Reich would be foolhardy.

He believed the world had had its fill of death and destruction and it was now time to rebuild the cities and the towns, to create new technology, to harvest the lands and to build a bomb so destructive that anyone contemplating aggression towards the Third Reich would only bring about their own downfall. With many scientists in the clutches of Germany, Hitler had them working on weapons of mass destruction before the Allies could beat him to it. This was going to be Hitler's deterrent to any further nations waging war against Germany.

Hitler put a team of advisors together in order to persuade me as to what this manifesto should contain. I was told of the countries to visit, the cities to avoid, and particularly certain camps that were totally restricted. They would not have known what I the people from my timeline knew, but I was well aware of why I was given these strict orders and a strict guideline of where I could go throughout Europe. The Nazi High Command did not want to unmask their darkest secret, the death camps, which I knew by now they would be starting to dismantle once they had completed their final solution. I was given months of training and debriefing on what I was to document by so-called educators.

And so I was finally allowed to leave, and my first point of call was Berlin. I spent months there and was given travel and identity papers from Goebbels which allowed me to travel freely to capture the essence of German life under Nazi rule, always escorted, of course, by a couple of plain-clothes bodyguards. I knew damn well they were Gestapo. They watched everything I did and what I wrote in my diaries. Every night I had to hand it over for inspection to a major stationed in the Government district near the Reichstag. It was a beautiful city and I did find myself at times intoxicated by its power; each night after eating and drinking in its many vibrant bars and nightclubs I would go home and feel shame. It was a daily cycle from which I only found solace in drink. I would promise myself to stop, but each night I would drown out the shame in the bottom of a bottle. I met many high-ranking officials and officers during this time which allowed me access to inside information I otherwise would not have known, such as the way some German officers had been secretly keeping Jewish female slaves for their own sexual gratification under the guise of house-servants – something for which the SS would have shot them, had they found out. I kept that to myself to avoid any fingers being pointed in my direction. After some deep soul-searching and excessive drinking, I decided it was time to leave Berlin and move on.

Chapter 12
Old and New Friends

On February 13th 1943, I began my journey out of Berlin and my first destination was Paris. I knew I had to contact Sara and Eddie somehow. I needed to lose the two guards that followed me everywhere. They took turns sleeping in order to watch my every move. If I went to the bathroom, one always came with me, and even if I asked for privacy, the same old mantra was rattled out: *We are under strict orders from Berlin to protect you at all times.* I had to find a way to shake them off. I carried on my ruse of taking pictures of a new Europe and writing stories of what I had witnessed as the aftermath of the war took fold.

I had come up with a plan.

One problem I had wasn't *where* to meet Eddie and Sara. It was *when.*

While I was buried neck-deep with Hitler in the Wolf's Lair and all along the battlefront of his war, Sara and Eddie were busy photographing and filming in secret the new outcome of the war, and I only prayed that they were still alive and not rotting in some Gestapo jail being questioned as spies against the Reich. We had pre-arranged where we could meet after the war ended, but we did not know when it was going to end, so that was our main problem. If I could escape my minders in Paris and get a message to the owner of the Hotel Montholon, located at 15 Rue Montholon, just off Rue La Fayette, it would give me a chance to connect with them eventually. A loose plan, but it was all I had. The hotel owner was a resistance sympathiser and if I could just get there, I could find out if my fellow time-travelling friends had made contact with him. If not, I could hold up there and await their return. In the meantime, I could capture my own written accounts and at the very least would keep up appearances if any other suspicious Gestapo came calling. But for now, it was time to lose my two so-called bodyguards.

I had in my possession documents giving me the freedom of Germany and its new colonies, on top of a recent photograph of me shaking hands with Adolf Hitler.

I think any Nazi police wishing to doubt my credentials would soon be scuttling away in fear, assuming me to be some high-ranking figure in the Nazi party. I just hoped I wouldn't be taken or shot by any remaining French resistance fighters still active not knowing who I really was. The stakes were high, and I was eager to find my two lost friends.

On the 16th of February 1943, I arrived in Paris as the steam train screeched to a halt in the Gare du Nord. The call was made to disembark. All I had was my side satchel containing my travel documents, identification papers, writing notes and a small suitcase with a change of clothes suitable for the period I now found myself in. My two goons followed closely behind me. German soldiers lined the platforms every ten meters. I got off the train and stopped to look up to see the high metal beams crossing the wide expanse of the station's roof. I then started to move and made my way down the crowded platform to exit through the end gate where the usual queues developed with Gestapo and SS soldiers checking papers before allowing people through. It came to our turn, and after the usual head-to-toe visual screening without so much as a smile, the stern-looking Gestapo gentleman in his leather jacket nodded me to move on and I was ushered through without question. My bodyguards were ushered through in turn. I made my way up the metal staircase with other travellers and out into the Paris atmosphere. It appeared relaxed but busy. It had started to rain, and the ground was wet with only a few leaves strewn on the pavements. People scuttled along this way and that with bowed heads trying to avoid the rain drops that were falling down. Or maybe their bowed heads were in fact for other reasons. As birds flew above oblivious to the new world that now graced our skies, my eyes wandered around in appreciation of this beautiful city and its architectural grandeur until my eyes fell upon the numerous red and black Swastika flags hanging in triumph outside every building. The SS was here, and they ensured everyone knew about it. I also knew that it would be a sight beheld in every German-controlled city around Europe. I took some photos to keep up my hidden secret and, wanting to escape,

I heaved a sigh and began my walk of shame along the streets of Paris until I found myself standing at the most famous of all Parisian streets: the Champs Elysées. In the distance, I could see the SS flags blowing triumphantly on the Eiffel Tower, which I can only assume was a horrific eyesore to all Parisians. I watched as people walked around in a daze as German troops marched up and down in patrols along the Champs Elysées. Many uniformed officers sat around and drank coffee unhindered under marquees in cafés and bars and on side streets as if it had always been that way. As the rain started to ease, I could see the arrogant look on the faces of German officers barking orders for service at the put-upon French waiters. For now, it was something they would have to endure. Indeed, the whole of Europe would have to endure this new Nazi regime and hope and pray for some kind of salvation which may never come.

But maybe, just maybe I would be able to right this wrong. For now, I had to get to Hotel Montholon on La Fayette.

As I walked along a side street, I was stopped in my tracks by a very pretty French girl who was wearing only a silk nightgown, French knickers and high heels. "Allo, mister, you want to come in and play?" she asked me in her French accent. The two goons still by my side laughed to themselves as they looked this scantily-clad lady up and down. I realised it was a hooker; an attractive one at that.

"Ah, no, thank you," I politely declined.

"Ah no, why, don't you like pretty girls?" she asked me. The two guards just shook their heads as if in disbelief, but then it came to me. This could be my chance to slip my German shadows.

"Maybe I could come in for a little while, if that's okay?" I said to her.

"Ah yes, indeed, come in and bring your friends too," she said.

I followed her in, and my 'friends' followed after me.

The place was dimly lit with old lamps, some of them with red scarfs thrown over for them for effect. Soon other girls came over and started to paw at my two German minders as they were escorted over to the bar. There was one staircase leading up. I looked up at it and thought that could be my way out.

"Would you like to buy me a drink?" my new lady friend asked. "My name is Rochelle. What is your name?"

"John," I replied.

"It's nice to meet you, John."

I got to the bar and ordered a bottle of red wine and said to Rochelle, "Why don't we take this upstairs?"

"Sure, why not?" she replied in fairly good English. As I was about to head up, one of the goons grabbed my arm and ordered me to "make it quick."

"Not too quick, I hope," Rochelle quipped in reply, with a sexy grin on her face.

He let go of me and let out a little grunt. She linked my arm and led me up the stairs. He went back to the bar and ordered drinks for himself and his buddy and three other ladies closed in around them, hoping for some business to come their way.

Rochelle led me to the second room at the top of the stairs. She opened the door and I walked in. She closed the door behind her, and locked it. "So, do you want to pay in dollars or francs?" she asked.

"Look, I will pay you for your time, but I need your help. I need to get out of here, alone," I said.

"You don't want to have fun with me?"

"It's not that – I need to get away from those two gentlemen downstairs," I told her.

"I see," she said.

"Can you help me?" I pleaded.

"Okay – at the end of the hallway, there is a fire escape. You can make your way out onto the lane which leads back out onto the street," she informed me.

"Thank you, Rochelle," I said.

I started to take out some money when she said, "No, it's okay, just go."

"Are you sure? I'm more than happy to pay you for your time, for helping me at least," I said.

"I charge for sex, John, not helping someone get away from the Germans," she replied. I nodded and smiled at her in appreciation. "Let me check outside first." She went to the door, opened it carefully and stuck her head out to look around. She crept out and I followed her to the door. She went to the top of the stairs and peeked down then looked back at me and told me to go. I waved at her and headed to the end of the hallway. I came to a door and I turned the handle to open it. I looked out and there were the stairs leading down. Just then I heard a shout from the bar below.

"Hey, you, lady, what are you doing there?" said one of my German minders. He had seen her at the top of the stairs.

"Go," she shouted to me. I ran down the staircase and pushed open a door and found myself in a lane. From upstairs, I could hear commotion and people screaming. It sounded like a mix of Rochelle and one of my goons. I didn't hesitate and ran out onto the street. As much as I hoped they didn't hurt the girl, I needed to get away – saving humanity was a higher priority.

I ran as fast as I could east of my location and ducked into a shop doorway and looked back to see if I was being followed.

Then I saw the two men. One crossed the other side of the street, while one stayed on my side and started to hurry down towards my hiding place. When they didn't change direction, I turned and pushed into the shop. As I found my bearings inside, I noticed it was a gent's suit store. I grabbed a jacket and headed for a dressing room and pulled over the curtain. There were two other men getting fitted and a shop clerk asked me something in French. I didn't understand and just stuck up my thumb. I peeked through the curtain and could see one of the men run past the shop window. I waited for about another five minutes before coming out. I put the jacket back on the rail and slowly headed to the door. I heard something in French again but I just waved them away and opened the door to look outside. Looking left and right, I could not see the men; finally, I had lost them. I quickly left and continued down the road and disappeared down a side street, I tucked in behind a wall and pulled out a map I had.

Checking the map, I worked out roughly where I was and started a five-mile trek across the city.

The skies were still grey and unlikely to brighten as it was now evening, and the Parisian lights were starting to be lit. For someone from the year 2003, it was a truly amazing experience to watch people of this era go about their business like everything was normal. But then again, apart from the occupation, everything to them was normal. I was the stranger here. The outsider, the time-travelling, history-changing co-conspirator who brought havoc on the world. I watched as men and women peddled by on bicycles, that were not that different to what you would see on the cobble-stoned streets of Amsterdam in my own time. It felt surreal. I had to keep moving, I needed to make contact with the hotel and hope to God that I would not be mistaken for a traitor. The only way that was going to happen was to hope Eddie and Sara had been there and informed the owner of my pending arrival. Failing that, I knew I was a dead man.

I passed the many famous galleries of Lafayette and the beautiful Haussmann building with its sophistication and splendour: the neo-byzantine dome, whose stained-glass windows diffused a myriad of multi-coloured lights, a stunningly beautiful building, now trapped in Nazi clutches.

After staying on as many side streets as possible and avoiding main areas, I eventually neared the hotel. I scanned the road and waited for twenty minutes to see who was coming and going. I did not see German uniforms enter or leave at any time.

Eventually, I had to move: standing here all night would look suspicious to either side. I was also fearful of my two German minders catching up with me.

I pulled my jacket in tight and walked across the road towards the hotel entrance. With one final glance around, I took a breath and entered through the wood and glass door.

The hotel had a rustic old charm to it, and a lady was standing behind the counter. She was about fifty with shoulder-length blonde hair. She was short at about five foot two inches and wore a flowered pattern dress and as she looked at me, I could sense her suspicious looks.

"*Bonjour,*" she said.

"*Bonjour,*" I said back, and she immediately knew I wasn't French.

"Can I help you?" she said, in English.

I was surprised, and I said, "I'm looking for a room for a few days, please."

"Identity papers, please," she said as she held out her hand. I reached into my satchel and took out my papers and handed them over. This was standard practice for hotels in occupied territories. She looked them over and handed them back to me, then asked for my passport. I gave it to her.

"I need to hold this for inspection for the police," she said. Knowing this to be the norm, I just nodded in agreement. "You will get them back when you check out."

"*Merci*," I said, hoping it would soften her face – it didn't.

She told me to follow her and she led me up a flight of stairs to room 10, at the end of a hallway. She opened the door and led me in. "Bathroom is there," she pointed. "We stop serving food at 7:30pm, if you're hungry."

"Thank you."

She handed me the key, nodded, and left the room closing the door behind her. I walked to the window and checked the street in both directions but didn't see anything untoward. I went and sat on the bed, flopped back and stared at the worn wooden-beamed ceiling with its floral-patterned design. It needed repainting. The walls had wallpaper peeling and there was a musty smell in the air. Since the start of the war, money was tight, and decoration was not a priority.

One light bulb hung down in the centre of the room and there were used candles dotted around the room. A box of matches lay on the bedside table. I got up, took the matches and lit just a couple of candles. I went to the bathroom and splashed water from the rusty tap onto my face. I dried off with a towel hanging on the back of the door and decided I would nap for an hour before going down for food. I took off my boots and lay back on the bed. I fell asleep soon after.

I awoke suddenly to the sound of a barking dog outside. Checking my pocket watch, I realised it was after ten and I had missed my option for food.

I got up, put on my boots, freshened up and headed down to the hotel reception. No one was there. The hotel had a bar just to the right of the reception area and I heard people chattering. I slowly made my way in through a doorway and into the bar. People stopped talking and stared at me. I just nodded and said, "Hello." They returned to their chattering without acknowledging me.

"Do you want a drink?" the barman said, looking in my direction.

"Yes, please," I said gratefully.

"My wife, Edith, told me you checked in earlier," the large stocky Frenchman said. He was a little older than his wife, maybe late fifties, and still had all his hair albeit a little messy and greasy. He had a small scar about two inches long to his left cheek. Without asking me what I wanted, he poured me a small glass of red wine and said, "*Salut.*"

I returned the comment and knocked it back in one. He poured again. This time I let it sit.

"I'm afraid our kitchen is closed, but if you are hungry, I'm sure we could whisk you up some cheese and bread," he said.

"Sure, that would be fine, thank you," I replied. He nodded and went around the back to prepare the food.

I picked up the glass of red wine and took a sip. I could feel the glances in my direction as the people in the bar kept murmuring to themselves. There were ten people in the bar sitting around old wooden tables and chairs. A group of four older men sat together, two younger couples sitting near the window were giggling amongst themselves and in the far corner to my right of the bar one table of two men who were not talking at all. These two made me feel uneasy. I sat on a stool and waited for the owner to return, which he did after about five minutes, and in his hands was a large plate with a baguette, cut in half, with large chunks of cheese inside. I was quite hungry and was happy to have anything at all. "Thank you so much, Mr...?" I paused waiting for him to reply.

"My name is Henri Lamont. I am the owner of the hotel and bar, and my wife Edith looks after the rooms and kitchen," he informed me.

"Thank you, Henri, for the food," I said, as I took a large bite into the cheese baguette. He smiled and returned to tending his bar, cleaning glasses and checking on the other patrons.

As I took the last bite of the roll, the two men who had been quietly sitting in the corner got up and whispered something to Henri and then left, leaving money for the bill on the table. I watched them leave as one looked back as he exited the side door. Henri looked at me and returned behind the bar.

"Do you know those men?" I asked.

"Friends," is all he said. I didn't reply and finished my drink. I sat there for another hour as Henri kept pouring as if he didn't want me to leave. As the last patrons left, he locked the side door and pulled down all the curtains that faced out onto the street.

I got up to leave to return to my room, when Henri said, "Wait there."

"Why?" I asked.

"Please, John, just wait here for two moments," he insisted. He went back into the kitchen at the back and I decided to take a look around through the curtains to see if anyone was watching or waiting for me. I felt very nervous now, and my mind raced with the thoughts of who those two men where and what they had whispered to Henri. Were they Gestapo? Maybe my two minders had reported me missing and put out an alert with local police.

Maybe it was worse. Could they be French resistance on the hunt for Nazi sympathisers? An easy target alone in a French bar. I grew more tense as I started to toy with the idea of bolting out the side door.

Taking one more look outside and seeing an empty street I decided to run. As I pulled back the bolt on the wooden door, I heard, "Where do you think you are going?" I stopped dead. Frozen in fear, I couldn't move. And then it dawned on me – it was a voice I recognised.

I slowly turned around, and there she was. That smile, that face. It was her; it was Sara.

"You made it!" she said in her beautiful Italian accent. I ran to her and we wrapped our arms around each other tightly then tilted our heads back and started laughing in unison.

"God, I am so happy to see you, Sara," I beamed.

"Me too," she replied.

Just then Henri came back in and went to lock the door again. "Hurry, out the back," he said, ushering us out. He turned out the bar lights and we made our way into his hotel kitchen. There was a large wooden table in the middle and he told us to sit down. Sara was a sight for sore eyes. I couldn't stop staring at her. I felt relieved too. Not only that she was alive, but I finally had a friendly face to look at, something I had not seen for quite some time.

"Where's Eddie?" I shouted out, nearly forgetting about him as I immersed myself in Sara.

"He's okay. He's making his way back from Milan and should be here in two or three days. We got separated there about four weeks ago as the Gestapo were almost onto us. We travelled separately for a while and we said we'd meet back here in a few weeks. According to Henri's contacts, he's okay and will return soon," she finished.

"I'm just so glad to see you're okay," I repeated. She just smiled and placed her hand on mine.

"We need to plan our return, John, our way back home," she urged. "We need to get to Berlin, find young Doctor Hoitdle and get the hell out of this living nightmare."

"I totally agree," I replied, and we got down to the discussion of how and when. When Eddie returned, we could gather our evidence and make the journey back to Berlin to locate Hoitdle and show him how BETI really worked so he could send us back to 2003.

It seemed a million miles away; yet another crazy plan, but for now I was just so happy to spend some time with Sara in Paris, the city of love. *Thank god for small mercies*, I thought. For now, I would soak up Paris, share our stories, and most of all I would embrace my time with Sara.

One night while out walking in the city of love, Sara was speaking to me about their many travels and scary adventures but one stuck out for me. It was their time in Prague.

Chapter 13
Prague

"EDDIE, EDDIE, LOOK OVER THERE," Sara told her fake husband while pointing down a cobbled street off the main Prague square, Wenceslas.

The border regions collectively known as the Sudetenland of Czechoslovakia had been occupied by the German army since 1938, with the intention of expanding in time. Then on the 15th of March 1939, the German Wehrmacht had marched into the rest of the country and Hitler had made a triumphant entry into Prague that very evening.

The country had been under martial law and the rounding up of the Jewish population was a primary goal of one man: Reinhard Heydrich. He was a high-ranking German SS officer and a principal orchestrator of the Holocaust. He had been responsible for the deportation of all Jewish people from Europe. He had been given his name the *man with the iron heart* by Adolf Hitler himself. This was a dangerous place for Eddie and Sara to be wandering out in.

"Christ, what are they going to do with those women?" Eddie replied. As they both looked down the street, Eddie began secretly filming. Four SS soldiers had lined up ten women against a wall and were stripping them of their clothes and their dignity. Passers-by were quickly ordered away and obeyed without hesitation.

"Sara, try to look like you're posing for a picture," Eddie asked.

"Make it quick, there are too many soldiers patrolling the streets here," Sara replied with fear in her throat.

"That's it, hold it there," he told her. With Sara posing as if to try take in the background of the buildings, Eddie caught the whole thing on film.

The guards had the women down to their underwear— some of them were left exposed from the waist up—and Sara and Eddie could hear them crying and desperately begging for mercy. The guards were laughing, and all the women could do was hope for a miracle. Then the shots started. One by one, the guards took it in turn to shoot the women with their rifles; their cruelty knew no bounds, as they deliberately shot them in parts of their bodies that would not kill them instantly, their arms, legs, shoulders, and even in the groin. The blood poured from their bodies as they fell to the ground in agonising pain. In the surrounding buildings doors and windows were slamming shut. No one would be coming to their aid.

After more callous laughter, the SS men took out their sidearms and eventually put a bullet in their brains until the last woman stopped screaming.

"I think I'm going to be sick," Sara cried as she doubled over retching in the street and hurled into the gutter. Eddie turned his camera away quickly and focused on getting Sara up and away.

Eddie noticed one of the soldiers looking his way.

"You okay, Sara, you okay to move? We better leave, right now," he asked. With that, she nodded her head, straightened up and they both began to walk away.

As they headed back down Wenceslas Square to make their way towards the small innocuous hotel where they had been staying, they heard the all-too-familiar shout: "*Halt, halt.*" It was the soldier who had been looking at Eddie a few moments ago.

Eddie looked over his shoulder and told Sara to keep on walking. He was about forty feet away and the other three soldiers were further back up the street where they had originally filmed. "Keep moving; as soon as we get to the next corner, take it and run."

"Halt!" the SS man shouted again, and just as he took his rifle from his shoulder to fire a warning shot, they hit the next street and they both ran. They scarpered as fast as they could, trying not to twist an ankle on the cobble stones. They could hear the whistles of the SS soldier as he tried to summon and alert any other soldier in the area to come and aid his search.

Eddie shoved and pushed Sara along through every turn and side street they came to in an attempt to avoid being caught with evidence. With a few more turns they could hear in the distance the whistle become faint and they broke into a walk and stepped into a dark alley not far from Charles Bridge. The bridge crossed the Vltava river and led to Prague Castle, now being occupied and used as the headquarters of the German SS and by Reinhard Heydrich.

Gasping for air and working out the stitches in their bodies, Eddie stuck his head around the corner to check they were not being followed.

"Let's find a café or beer hall to sit tight for a few hours and let the patrol run out of steam before we return to the hotel," Sara advised.

They edged out slowly and left the lane, making sure no soldiers were around, then walked a few hundred metres back towards the old square but stayed off the main streets to try avoiding patrols. There were a few drunk soldiers roaming around, but they paid no heed to them. They eventually came to a café bar about a five-minute walk from their hotel. Looking up at the sign as Eddie opened the door, it read *Kavarna Praha*.

There were a few patrons sitting around the café and Sara went to order some hot drinks. Eddie had to keep up the premise of a mute; you never knew who was listening. Spies were all over occupied Europe.

"Prosím, prosím, dvě kávy (two coffees please)," Sara asked. An unsmiling waiter standing behind the bar just grunted something, and went off to pour the coffee from an old metal kettle before placing the cups on a tray. He added a small jug of milk and a

ceramic bowl of sugar with two teaspoons and brought them over to a table Eddie had picked out by the window of the cafe, where they could watch the street. One by one, the waiter took the items off the tray and walked away without saying a word.

"Friendly guy," Eddie whispered.

"Yeah, Czech people aren't renowned for their love of outsiders," Sara replied.

"From what we just witnessed, could you blame them?" Eddie said in a low voice, trying not to be heard.

"No, I guess not," Sara agreed.

They took little sips of their coffee and sat back to take a breath and process what they had just witnessed. They sat there for some time in silence, just watching out the window for search patrols, as customers came and went.

Two hours passed, and they decided to get up and go. Eddie left money on the table and they went out onto the street after nodding farewell to their not-so-friendly waiter. Looking up and down the street they made the short journey back once again along the famed cobblestoned back streets to the edge of the Old Square.

There were a few people coming and going but mainly soldiers and officers walking the square and checking out cafes and taverns to see where they could sample the local craft beers; and, of course, for some of the enlisted men to check out the local women. Their hotel was about sixty feet away, on the corner of the square, and they headed out arm in arm, with Sara putting on a fake laugh to try and look like any normal couple out on the town. Eddie had his camera over his shoulder and did his best to keep it out of sight behind his back. They had a few soldiers nod in their direction but they eventually arrived safely back at their hotel.

With a final glance out around the square, they went inside and straight to the reception counter to ask for their room key. A pretty girl of about nineteen took the large key off a hook behind her and passed it over with just a shy smile and a nod exchanged. They headed up the narrow winding stairs and arrived on the second floor; they went inside and locked the door behind them.

"We need to leave tomorrow, it's just too dangerous to stay around here," Eddie said. Sara agreed, and they decided to leave in the morning as soon as they had breakfast.

As usual on their travels Sara took the large double bed and Eddie graciously put himself in the not-so-large armchair, wrapping himself in an itchy woollen blanket pulled from the top shelf in the wardrobe to try to keep warm.

The room was average size, and six wooden beams ran across the ceiling, with wallpaper in between. The wardrobes were mahogany and matched the double bed. Their room was to the rear of the hotel, and the two bedroom windows were covered with cream net curtains. They overlooked a narrow street that appeared to be used for market sellers, judging by the empty stalls left there overnight.

Eddie put his hands to his lower back, let out a long aching noise and said, "Next time, I'm in the bed and you can sleep on the chair. I'm getting too old for this."

Sara took pity on him and, feeling a little guilty for always having the comfy bed replied, "Eddie, get in the bed. You'll sleep better."

Eddie looked up, surprised, from his uncomfortable chair and itchy blanket and asked, "Really?"

"Yes, but keep your hands to yourself, and keep to your side. No funny business or you'll be out one of those windows," Sara replied quickly.

"Don't worry, you're not my type," Eddie replied.

"Oh? And why is that?" Sara enquired out of curiosity.

"You're far too bossy for me. I like my women tame," Eddie quipped.

"Oh, I'm sure you do, Eddie. Now come on, let's get some sleep and get out of Prague and on to Paris," Sara said, while tapping the bed to invite him in. Eddie stripped down to his undergarments as did Sara. Eddie did take a few sneaky glimpses in Sara's direction as he got into the bed and pulled back the covers, but she gave him a stern look and he turned his head away and put his head on the pillow facing the opposite direction. They both drifted off to sleep on separate sides of the bed.

The next morning Eddie and Sara were awoken to the sound of vehicles outside. Eddie got up and ran to the window, to see two army transport trucks, with about eight soldiers from each exiting to the sounds of a German officer yelling orders.

"Get dressed quick, security checks outside," Eddie told Sara. They both scrambled for their clothing and dressed as fast as they could. They did up their boots and grabbed their equipment and bags and headed out of the bedroom towards the stairs. They took a few steps down when the front door of the hotel was pushed open hard by an SS officer, who ordered his men inside. The officer went straight to the reception and demanded to see the register from the young Czech girl who was standing nervously behind the counter. She quickly obeyed and pulled out the register book from under the desk and slid it sheepishly over to the officer. With a death stare, he looked at her for a few moments and then finally spun the open book around to inspect the names occupying the rooms. He asked for the passports being held by the hotel and the girl turned around and, using a key from her apron pocket, opened a drawer on a cabinet behind her, took out seven passports and handed them over. The SS officer started looking through each one while his men stood and waited for instructions.

"What do you think, Sara?" Eddie asked.

"Well, our documents are in order. Maybe we should play it cool and act normal, stick to our plan and hope they're just doing routine checks?" Sara said.

"Or we could make a run for it. Find another way out of here and not take the risk at all," Eddie suggested, shrugging his shoulders.

With that the SS officer shouted orders to his men and they immediately began running up the stairs and started knocking on each door on the first floor.

"Quick, back inside, I have an idea," Sara ordered Eddie. They went back into the room and Sara told Eddie to put all their gear into the wardrobe. She opened her case and started throwing her clothes all over the room, making sure her lingerie was seen; a pair of knickers was left hanging off the end of the bed.

"What now?" Eddie asked.

"Quick, take all your clothes off," Sara demanded, as she started to strip off herself.

"What?" Eddie asked with a puzzled expression.

"Just do it, now," Sara said, strain apparent in her voice.

"Okay, if you insist."

Just as they were stripped naked, they heard the banging on the door.

"Quick, lie on the bed," Sara said. Eddie, realizing her plan, quickly jumped onto the bed and lay down flat on his back. Sara jumped on top of him.

Eddie looked at Sara and quipped, "Guess dreams do come true."

"One more word out of you, mute, and I'll give you up to the Germans myself."

Bang, bang, bang on the door – the SS officer was now demanding their door be opened. As they had left the door unlocked the officer twisted the knob and pushed the door open along with two of his men in tow.

"*Aagh, aagh, si, si,*" Sara called out, pretending to be lost in the moment as she grinded on top of Eddie. She swished her hair around as Eddie played up to it and kept his eyes closed, running his hands up and down her thighs and ass. Sara turned around quickly and jumped off Eddie with feigned shock and pulling a blanket over herself and leaving Eddie exposed.

The SS officer, taken aback, said immediately in German, "Oh, excuse me madame, sorry to interrupt," and—after momentarily enjoying the glimpse of Sara's naked body—ordered his men back outside.

"Please, get dressed and come outside for identity check," the officer said.

Sara keeping up her guise, nodded and in Italian, said, "Yes, sir."

The officer took a last glance at her and left the room to wait outside as his men continued with their checks in the other rooms.

Eddie got dressed and Sara just put on a silky dressing gown, making sure to reveal part of her cleavage as she brought their identity papers to the officer waiting outside. The officer, trying to avoid looking straight down at her breasts, introduced himself as SS-Sturmbannführer, Major Franz Kronig, an SS assault unit leader. He asked her first if she spoke German and then what their purpose was in Prague. Sara, able to speak a little German, was able to explain Eddie's mute condition and also their plans to take pictures to document the great expeditions of the growing German Empire. The officer looked over their papers and, despite his training to be suspicious of anyone not of German nationality, could see everything appeared to be in order. And then came an unusual request.

"Madame Letari, could I ask you, if it's not too much trouble… Would you take a picture of me and my men?"

Sara, feeling relieved to have passed their first real test under scrutiny, of course agreed, and the officer ordered his men to stand close to the top of the stairs with himself at the very front. Sara went and retrieved her camera ,and walking back out still in her silky gown, gave a cheeky smile to all the soldiers who were enjoying looking her up and down. Eddie just came to the bedroom door and watched in amazement at how easily men fell for a pretty girl. Sara told all the men to smile and then took the photo, and for good measure took a second one for luck to make it look all so normal.

The officer thanked Sara. "Maybe you will publish that in the newspaper or a book one day, and say we are the proud fighting SS men of the Third Reich."

"Major Kronig, it would be my pleasure to add you and your fine men to our documented travels and tell people how gracious and handsome you all were," Sara said sincerely. The officer clicked his heels together and, with a bend of his head to Sara and a knowing glance to Eddie, gave a right-handed Nazi salute into the air and shouted, "*Heil Hitler.*"

Sara repeated, "*Heil Hitler,*" while Eddie—playing the mute—just gave the arm salute. The officer ordered his men down and out, and he followed quickly after.

Sara walked to the edge of the stairs and waited until she heard the door close. She turned to Eddie and smugly strolled back past him into the bedroom.

"Okay, okay, nicely played. This time. But not all SS men will be like him. We need to get to Paris, now," Eddie said, and Sara agreed. Eddie looked out of the window and saw the two vehicles drive away.

They once again packed up and made their way downstairs to check out. They paid their bill, retrieved their passports from the young girl, and headed off to find a bus to the train station.

Within ten minutes, they had found a bus packed with commuters that would take them the short journey to *Praha Masarykovo nádraží,* Prague Masaryk railway station, where they could take connecting trains to Paris. Despite how much they had been travelling around Europe, it was always surreal to them to be travelling on something that could be straight out of a 1940s Hollywood movie.

They arrived at the station and Sara went to buy the train tickets. Eddie took a seat by a wooden bench further down the platform. It was slightly damp, and Eddie used his hand to push away any residual dampness before sitting down.

Once Sara had the tickets, she placed them in her bag and started to walk towards Eddie.

Suddenly two men stood out in front of her and she knew exactly who they were by the way they were dressed: the long brown trench coat, pin striped trousers and black shiny shoes.

Gestapo.

"Nationality?" they asked of Sara.

"Italian," she replied. The usual antics started, and they asked her for her papers. Eddie who was wistfully nodding along to a tune in his head turned to his right to look for Sara and then seeing the situation, stood up and caught her eye. While the two Gestapo men were looking at her papers, Sara gave Eddie a look as if to say *stay calm, everything is alright.*

Other people hurried by to avoid being harassed. It was common for everyone to be fearful of the Gestapo, as they could stop and arrest you for any minor thing.

One of the men, who was a little taller than the other, reached into his inside pocket and pulled out a picture and showed it to Sara.

He asked her, "Have you seen this man?" Her eyes almost watered as she saw the likeness of Eddie. It was not a photograph, but a pencil-drawing of a man resembling Eddie. It was not exact, but the curly hair and the oval face was close enough to be alarming.

"I don't know him," she said, in deliberately broken German.

"We did not ask if you know him, Fräulein, we asked you if you have seen him," the smaller man now asked.

"Eh, no, sorry, I have not seen him," she tried to say in half-German and half-Italian, hoping they would go away in irritation at her poor attempts to translate. They both looked her up and down and the man with the picture put it away again and started to gaze around.

Sara caught Eddie's eye again and managed to give him a meaningful look. *Go. Go now.* He looked at her for a moment, saw the look of fear on her face and knew. He turned his face away and started to walk further away from her towards the end of the platform. The two men waved her on, and Sara decided to wait at a different bench from Eddie until the men left the area. However, the two men had started to walk down towards Eddie's position.

Sara looked up at a large clock on the platform and saw the train was due in three minutes.

Eddie turned left in towards the station building to duck out of sight, but the men kept walking in his direction.

He went inside and scanned the station and spotted the men's toilet and ran over to it. Sara, not knowing what was going on, picked up her case and started walking down toward the two Gestapo men.

It appeared the men had seen something as they had quickened their step and headed to the same entrance Eddie had gone in.

Entering the toilet, Eddie went straight into the last of five cubicles and locked the door with its flimsy lock.

The Gestapo men arrived at the station entrance and decided to split up. The smaller of the two headed back up towards the ticket booths where Sara had first bought the tickets, while the taller man stayed near the toilets. After looking around at different areas of the station and seeing nothing, his eyes paused at the toilets and headed over to check them out. Sara arrived at the entrance and looked to see what was going on. She saw the Gestapo officer walk into the toilets and she feared the worst. There was not much she could do now. She went back outside and waited. The train was due in one minute.

Eddie heard someone come inside. He stood still in the cubicle and waited silently. Thump; Eddie heard the first toilet door being pushed open. Then the second. Eddie lifted his feet up onto the toilet and stayed in a crouched position. The third door was opened, and then the fourth.

He felt he was done for.

The German pushed at the fifth door and it would not open. He tried it again and saw it was locked. Sweat was starting to roll down Eddie's back and he tried to figure out how to get out of this situation.

Realizing he had no other choice, he decided to make a move. He undid the lock slowly with his fingers and waited.

The tall man bent down to look under the toilet door and this time Eddie was standing on the floor. With that Eddie flung open the door and rushed the officer and pushed him hard up against the tiled wall behind him, catching him off-guard and dazing the officer. Eddie grabbed his head and slammed it two, three, four times against the hard wall, then kneed him in the groin. The officer fell to the ground in pain and Eddie proceeded to kick him four or five times in the head until he stopped moving; still breathing, but unconscious. Eddie ran his hands back through his hair and straightened himself up when he heard someone walk in. It was just another passenger, an older gentleman who stared down at the man on the ground and as Eddie was about to protest, the man started yelling in German, "Help, police, police!"

Eddie panicked and looked for a way out. He turned around and at the back of the toilet was a window about five feet off the ground. He went to it quickly and found he could push it open. He looked around and saw it opened onto a stone gravel yard where old train carriages and tracks lay abandoned. He jumped up and slid his way out and into the yard and pushed the window closed behind him.

Sara, outside on the platform, heard whistles and two police officers running from halfway down the station, and knew where they were heading. She heard the screeching breaks of the train pulling up at the platform and panicked, not knowing what to do. She hurried to the edge of the platform and waited for the train to pull up.

Eddie ran over to one of the disused carriages and hid behind it while thought about his next moves. He could see the very end of the platform, and quickly made his way there to see if he could spot Sara.

The train pulled in and Sara waited and waited. Five more police officers had arrived on the scene and were frantically looking around the platforms and running in and out of the station. The shorter Gestapo officer who had arrived at the scene had come out onto the platform and was barking orders to the police officers sending them this way and that to hunt down the assailant.

Sara heard the final call to board, and reluctantly decided she had to board. Eddie could be caught. She had to go; Eddie would understand. He was probably on the run now. She got on board and a train inspector closed the door behind her. The final whistle was sounded, and she could hear the steam engine starting to roar as the train pulled away from the platform. She pushed down the window on the door and looked outside. It was good to put distance between her and the policemen but she feared the worst for Eddie. She was about to go and find a seat when she saw him. He had run along a grassy edge where the disused sleepers lay and made his way to the fencing along the tracks. He was running alongside Sara's train, but the fence divided them.

"Eddie, what can I do?" she shouted.

He replied, "Nothing. Just make your way to Paris and I'll meet up with you at the rendezvous in a few days. I promise."

She shouted back through the noise of the train as it gathered speed, "Okay, Eddie, see you there. I'll wait as long as I can. Good luck!"

He could run alongside her no more. He waved her goodbye and slowed to a walk. She waved back and watched him as long as she could. He had turned and began to run back across the disused tracks as in the far distance police had started to comb the open yard area. As the train took a bend to the right, Eddie fell out of sight.

Sara picked up her belongings and headed for a seat in the passenger carriage. A Czech man travelling with a little girl helped her with her bags and placed them in an overhead rack for her. She sat down and looked out of the window as the world flashed by, and prayed Eddie would escape capture and make it to Paris to reunite the team once again.

Chapter 14
The Way Back

As the last night with Sara grew to a close, I knew it was time to focus on getting home. I had spent five wonderful carefree days and nights with Sara, and Eddie had returned as promised just the morning before our last day.

He was sure he was on the radar of the Gestapo. Eddie believed the soldiers they witnessed murdering the ten women may have given a description to the Gestapo; if they suspected he was taking pictures of it, they could be hunting him to destroy the evidence.

I was horrified, but not surprised, to hear Sara's stories of travelling with Eddie. It made my stomach churn, as I too felt implicit in giving Hitler his victories. The guilt we all carried was etched permanently in our memories. But we had a job to do and for now we had to put that aside to move onto the next part of our perilous mission.

We needed to act fast. With Henri's help, and the aid of the resistance, we all managed to get the last train safely out of Paris on the fifth night.

We were heading back into the lion's den, to Berlin. I used my papers hoping my two dumped goons had not given me away. I believed the last thing they would do would be to inform their superiors that they had lost me; Berlin did not appreciate failure. I still had strong links in Berlin and solid travel papers, so no one questioned me or the two people who were with me. I said they were documenting the great Nazi regime, and this seemed to stop all further questioning.

With the war finally won, there appeared to be less paranoia amongst the Germans and our travel back was for the most part unhindered.

In our own private car on the train, Eddie was able to show me some of the incredible visions across Europe he and Sara had captured. He was like a kid in a candy store with what he had filmed in all its full-colour glory. Moving pictures and sounds of World War Two, with modern day technology to bring it to vivid reality.

He showed me one particular event from November 14th, 1941. Eddie was with Sara filming in a small town just outside Brussels called Dinant.

"It was one of the most picturesque towns in the region," Sara said smiling.

"The winding river valley and beautiful buildings of Dinant looked like they were straight out of a fairy-tale," Eddie added. They had been near the cliff face when Eddie caught on film a commotion at the top of the cliff: at the very top, sat the citadel, a fortress overlooking the town now held by the Germans and used by the SS to bring prisoners-of-war or local dissidents. As he filmed, he saw a blindfolded man being brought to the edge of the cliff, flanked by two SS guards and a man in plain clothes who stood behind him, most likely Gestapo. He appeared to be speaking to his prisoner. As they watched and waited in fear of what was going to happen, the plain clothes man kicked his leg forward to the back of the blindfolded man and sent him plummeting to his death. As his body splattered below, the ground rapidly ran red with blood. They quickly stopped filming after that and left the area in fear of being seen capturing a murder on film.

Not that there was anyone to bring the evidence to.

"It was horrible, John," Sara said in a sad voice. "But we have it all, the killings, the battles, the glorious but terrifying sight of marching armies in fallen cities. As horrific as it was to see, it was also a terrible beauty to witness."

I reached out to Sara and with the back of my hand I lightly caressed her face as she leaned into my touch.

We sat on the train in silence for hours as I took the time to look at all the still pictures Sara had taken. She was indeed a gifted photographer. As the clickety-click of the train rolled on and out of immediate danger, Sara fell asleep against the window and I watched her awhile. I then turned my gaze out the window and wondered how the hell we got here. I closed my eyes and tried to sleep but my mind kept wandering to Hoitdle and how we would get home.

We had two connections along our route, but we finally arrived back in Berlin at two in the afternoon, and we made our way out of the station and started the trek across Berlin to find young Hoitdle. We knew where to go, as Doctor Hoitdle from 2003 had told us where to find him in 1943: exactly where he was being held during the war, in that church bunker along with BETI.

We took a tram in from the train station in a thirty-minute journey across the city, a city standing tall in the midst of victory. We came to our final stop and got off the tram. We walked until we were at the edge of the right street, where we noticed it was quiet enough, and the area was not as occupied as Berlin's main district. We looked across the street and Eddie pointed out the old building about two hundred yards over.

It was an old, disused church located in the east of the city. It had an underground basement and the Germans had turned it into a lab for Hoitdle and his small team to work. They did not want to bring attention to what was going on underneath so only two plain-clothes guards roamed the grounds of the church. It wasn't like we could just break in and announce ourselves. I thought the best thing to do would be to wait. At some point, Hoitdle would have to come out either to smoke or just get air. Well, that's what we hoped would happen.

And so, we decided to wait. We found a small local café-bar back up the road from which we could just about see the church door through high metal gates with sharp metal points. Now, all we had to do was wait to see a young Hoitdle.

For three hours we drank coffees whilst German soldiers came and went. We did not want to look suspicious, so we started buying beers and told the barman it was a birthday celebration; Sara was the lucky girl, we decided.

There was little activity at the church, beyond a brief moment when a man appeared at the door to pass a note to one of the guards. As it started to get dark, we felt we needed to move before some SS officer decided to start asking us questions. Just as we were preparing to leave, I looked at the church entrance, and saw a spectacled man appear and light up a cigarette. He kept his head bowed and puffed away while kicking little stones off the ground.

"That's him," I told the others. They looked out and watched and then turned back to me.

"Are you sure?" Eddie said.

"I'm sure," I replied. "Okay, listen up: you two wait here. I'm going to go over and get his attention. I'll signal back to you if all is okay. If not, just run – don't try and rescue me or do anything stupid."

"Hey, we're relying on you too," Eddie replied in earnest.

"Good luck," Sara said and kissed me on the lips.

"Oh, don't mind me," Eddie said with a little hint of jealousy.

I got up and left the café and started walking towards the church gates. As I got nearer, one of the guards noticed me and started walking towards the gates. I was within about ten feet when the guard shouted "*Halt!*" and rambled on in German that I couldn't understand.

I looked around him and noticed the spectacled man looking at me. I took my chance.

"Doctor Hoitdle," I bellowed. He looked surprised and took a few steps back.

The guard pointed his machine gun at me, yelling and using his gun to point me away. "Doctor Hoitdle, I know about BETI," I yelled out. Just as the second guard appeared, the man in the doorway said, "Wait."

He spoke to the guards in German and they lowered their weapons. The tall spectacled man walked towards my direction and told one guard to open the gates.

"I am Doctor Hoitdle. How do you know me, and BETI?" he asked with a puzzled, inquisitive look.

"You told me about it," I replied with a wry smile.

"I don't recall ever meeting you – when did I ever tell you?" he asked.

I paused for a moment and said, "In 2003, you told me everything about BETI and my grandfather: Joseph Ryan."

He was taken aback and looked at me a while. "You'd better come inside."

"I have friends with me you need to see too," I said. He looked over my shoulder and I pointed back towards the café. "They are important to me, and to you."

He nodded in agreement. I turned back and waved to the café. Both Eddie and Sara appeared onto the street and walked towards us. The guards, looking nervous, turned to Hoitdle for guidance and he put out his hands in a reassuring gesture until they obeyed and stood down.

As they reached me, I introduced Sara and Eddie to Hoitdle, and he ushered us inside quickly before anyone noticed our little group. Hoitdle ordered the guards to keep eyes on the street and closed the large wooden door behind him.

"Follow me," he said. We went up the church past the altar and out to the back of the rectory through a doorway where there was a winding concrete stairwell that dropped thirty feet to a lower level. We came to another door and Hoitdle knocked out a sequence: three quick knocks followed by two slow ones. There was a shuffling inside, and the door bolted from the inside opened up. Two white-coated men looked at Hoitdle in puzzlement and he told them in German to relax. "These are my friends," he said. They looked at each other and one of them bolted the door shut again. A large wooden beam was then placed across the door for extra security.

My eyes turned to the room, and there it was: BETI.

A rather crude version, but nevertheless, there she was.

"So, are you going to tell me how you all got here, or do I have to beg?" Hoitdle asked.

"Doctor Hoitdle, I'm going to tell you everything – the whole goddamn ugly truth, and then when I'm done you're going to help us get home to 2003," I said sternly.

He looked at me and just said, "I am your humble servant and I wait with bated breath."

And so I did: Hoitdle heard it all, right from the very beginning. We showed him Eddie's and Sara's photos and film. He soaked it all in and sat in silence without any interruption about what his older self had planned and envisioned. His two whited-coated scientists sat back, too, with disbelief written all over their faces, but I could see Hoitdle believed it all. Why wouldn't he? He had been working on this from the very beginning. I finally told him how to make BETI work.

He let out a belly laugh. "Ha, your grandfather was always the smarter one," he beamed. "I loved him like a brother, you know. I miss him, and I wish he was here to see this…and you of course."

"Me too," I replied.

"Right, we need to get to work. Let's get you home – how does that sound, John?" he asked.

"That sounds good to me," I replied, and Sara and Eddie agreed.

"Good – then let's begin," Hoitdle said positively.

The dome was intact; a little dated-looking, but it appeared to have all the elements needed to send us back.

One of his white-coat assistants, a Czech national who was just called Arthuras, drew three vials of blood from my arm. The other assistant, a tubby short bald man in his fifties named Gerd Lokey, took one of the vials and inserted the missing link they had been waiting for into BETI's bio-tube and the data they needed started to pour out.

"It's working," Hoitdle said triumphantly

"That's a relief," Eddie said in his usual joking manner.

Sara added, "We need to start loading our evidence and equipment into the dome." Eddie picked up his equipment and assisted Sara in loading their hidden secrets and placed them on the metal floor inside.

The old button-style dials of the 1940s were being turned in sequence by Arthuras and Gerd. It was a far cry from the modern computer screens and scientific readings from 2003. But it was still functioning, and would get us home. The silver dome was the only feature that looked the same.

Hoitdle spoke to us once more and he was so proud and grateful to know that BETI worked. He thanked us all, and jokingly said, "Say hello to me when you get home!"

Once more, the three of us—Eddie, Sara and I—stood in front of our time machine and were once again saying goodbye to Doctor Hoitdle.

It was time to leave. We did not know what kind of world we were returning to, as we had changed so much history: Germany would be an empire, if Hoitdle's predictions were correct. We just needed to get back, and hand over the evidence. My job would be done. Eddie and Sara still had their work to be carried out, and I did not envy them one bit. They still had to document the different time periods and then finally, when everything had been captured, I was to be sent back to 1941 to undo our crimes. That seemed so daunting, and so far away; I was happy to put it to the back of my mind for now.

The team would be able to put together a remarkable piece of film to show the world what we had achieved, but in the end we knew we would have to destroy BETI. In the wrong hands, it could be used by madmen to destroy the world.

Young Doctor Hoitdle was so excited that he could hardly contain himself.

"Well, tell me, Mr. Ryan, how do I look for an old man in 2003?" he laughed.

"Not too bad at all," I replied.

"Ha, I look forward to seeing that in another sixty years so," he retorted.

"When we get back to the mansion with the coordinates your older self gave me, what guarantees will we have that it will be still there? What if other forces have taken it over, and we end up in lost in some time loop?" I asked, feeling unsure.

"Ah, good question, Mr. Ryan," he replied. "Now that we know that it has been a success, I will ensure, as soon as you depart tonight in BETI, that I obtain the mansion at all costs to guarantee it will be in our team's hands just as you left it. I give you my word," he said with sincerity.

"Okay – I guess our lives are in your hands now, Doctor Hoitdle," I said, looking around to Eddie and Sara who were listening intently.

"While we have sixty years to prepare for your arrival, it will only be seconds in your lifespan. Now let's get you back home. I'm sure you are looking forward to seeing old friends," Hoitdle said kindly.

Just as I was about to answer, there was a banging on the wooden doors of the lab. We all looked around at each other, and then at Hoitdle. He gestured, as if to say *be calm*, and walked over to the door.

Leaning in towards the door he said, in German, "Yes?"

One of the guards replied, "Doctor Hoitdle, you need to open the door. Captain Muller of the West Berlin Gestapo branch needs to speak with you," the guard replied. Hoitdle looked at his two assistants and told them to start the sequence to transport.

"You all need to move, now," he said in a quiet voice. Once again, the guard started to repeat his words, when Hoitdle stopped him halfway through and said, "One moment, please."

At that another voice interjected, presumably Captain Muller. "Open this door now, Doctor Hoitdle, or we will be forced to break it down. Please make things easier on yourself and your new friends."

My heart sank with those words. Someone outside knew we were here with Hoitdle. But who? Did the guards say something? Had someone been watching – maybe someone was onto Eddie after all? Or maybe the café owner got suspicious, and tipped off the local police. Either way, we needed to move, and move fast.

Arthuras told us to get into the dome and we obeyed immediately.

"This is your final warning," the Captain called from the other side of the door.

"I'm just getting the keys," Hoitdle shouted back through the door, trying to buy us time. With that there was a tat, tat, tat of machine gun fire around the locks. The door was so thick that it only had a slight effect, but we all jumped in fear. "Go, go," Hoitdle yelled to us.

He came running towards the doors of the dome. I came to the entrance and before I could say anything, he said, "Mr. Ryan, thank you for doing this, and thank you for showing us the way," and he held out his hand. I looked at his face and then his hand and reached out and firmly gave it a warm shake.

"What will they do to you?" I asked.

"Don't worry about me. I have friends that will see me out of this, and besides, I have a date with you all in sixty years! Now, go."

I turned and stepped back into the centre of the dome. The doors started to close, and we were left alone inside. We could hear the hum of BETI just like the first time, back at the mansion. We all eyed each other with wry smiles at what we had achieved, and waited to be transported home.

The intensity and the screaming of the dome started to surround our ears and vibrate through our bodies to the extent of passing out, just like back in 2003. Just as we were about to go, we heard a loud explosion from outside and the muffled sounds of shouting and screaming, and machine gun fire, and then, boom. Everything went black. After nearly two years.

We had gone. We had left 1943.

"You have done well my good Doctor; you have done very well indeed. Now the world will marvel at our achievements and cower at the mere sound of our name. No one could have predicted this outcome, and now we stand at the gates of former glory and the world will forever remember. And now you know what needs to be done, my old friend."

"Yes, it will be done as you command."

Chapter 15
Safe Haven

"Hey, wake up, John. John Ryan, can you hear me?" I heard the faint sounds of voices I did not recognise at first. My ears were still buzzing, and my vision was a little blurred.

A few moments later, my vision started to clear, and I found myself in a room I knew. I was back in the mansion and in the room I had been in before departure to 1941. A young nurse was holding a chart and she started to ask me again, "Can you hear me okay?" and I replied, "Yes, where are Eddie and Sara?"

"They are fine," she replied.

"Well, can I see them?" I asked as I went to get up and as I did, the nurse bellowed, "No, no, stay in bed, please," as I stumbled to the floor.

"Your legs are still a little weak, and you need to rest," she said, as she reached for my arm to help me back onto the bed.

I stayed sitting up and asked, "Where is Doctor Hoitdle?"

"I'm right here, Mr. Ryan," and there he was at the open doorway, beaming like a proud father. "You did it, you all did it."

"So, what does 2003 look like?" I asked.

"Exactly how we predicted, and so much more." He followed, "And when you are feeling up to it, you will see it all for yourself. But for now, you need to gather your strength. Sleep, eat, and then I will show you the new world."

"Okay. How're Eddie and Sara?" I asked again.

"Oh, they are just fine, resting up like you. You'll get to see them very soon; don't you worry about that, my young protégé," Hoitdle added. I nodded and lifted my feet back up onto the bed. "Nurse Muller here will take good care of you in the meantime. Anything you want, just ask." With that he left the room.

As I was about to put my head down on the pillow, I caught the figure of Hermann Leitman, the head of security and my driver from the airport. He stopped at the doorway, looked in towards me and without saying anything moved on after a moment's pause.

Gives me the creeps, I thought to myself.

"Can I get you anything?" the nurse asked. She was in her late thirties, curvy and very pretty. Her hair was dark, and tied back in a ponytail which ran through her cap. She had a mixed accent, and when I asked her where she was from, she said her mother was French and her father was German. She spoke softly and had a kind smile.

"Just water, please," I said, and with that she went to a nearby table and brought over two plastic bottles of water and a glass.

She left them by my bedside table and said, "Now rest."

"Thank you. Oh, what's your name by the way?" I quizzed.

"Noeline Muller," she replied.

"Well, thank you, Noeline," I said, smiling. She nodded, left the room and closed the door, leaving me to ponder on what I had just gone through. I wondered what the world was like, and most of all I thought of Sara. I wanted to see her face. I turned my head to the side and stared out the window into the dusky sky and with my eyes feeling heavy, I started to doze off and I fell into a slumber once more.

I woke up what must have been hours later, as it was dark outside. As I adjusted my eyes, I found myself still turned to the window. I then felt a presence in the room.

I turned my head around and sat up quick and indeed, someone was sitting by the side of the bed; it was Sara, beaming a glorious smile right in my direction.

"Hello, stranger," she said in that beautiful Italian accent of hers.

"Hello back," I said.

"I know it's been sixty years since I saw you last, but you still look very handsome for an old man," she said giggling to herself.

"Why, thank you, ma'am, you look as beautiful as always," I replied in a dumb American accent and with that she reached out to me and I in turn reached out to her and our faces met; we paused for a second then kissed for what felt like eternity. She got into the bed beside me, cuddled up into me and I held her tight. "Have you seen Eddie?" she asked.

"No, have you?"

"No, you are the first I've seen apart from Nurse Muller," she said.

"I'm sure he's fine. We can check on him on the way down," I said reassuringly.

I pulled her close to me and she placed her arm over my chest and ran it up to my face; we turned our heads to each other again and were about to kiss once more when we heard Leitman.

"Doctor Hoitdle wants to see you now." He stood there, waiting for a response. And he got one from Sara, "Okay, Mister Happy, we'll be right down."

I let out a little laugh and Leitman just stared back with an expressionless face and then left. As we heard his footsteps move away down the hallway, we looked at each with raised eyebrows and fell back onto the pillows in laughter.

We both got up and Sara went back to her room, to allow me to quickly freshen up and get changed into the new clothing that had been left for me on the chair. Looking out into the mansion's grounds, nothing looked any different from when I had left, although from my window it was hard to see much at all. I walked back to the bedside table, drank some water, left the room and entered the hallway. Sara's door was open and she looked ready to go; she saw me and smiled. Walking out to meet me she put her hand out to hold mine and I held it tight and we headed downstairs. We made our way back to the room in which I first met the team. It felt surreal being back and this time when we entered only Hoitdle and Leitman were waiting for us.

"Come in, come in please," Hoitdle said. "Sit, please." A butler entered the room. "Drinks! I think this calls for a celebration. Champagne please, Peter," he asked of the butler, who left. Leitman stood in the corner of the room and said nothing, but kept looking in our direction. I felt uneasy.

"Where is Eddie, Doctor Hoitdle?" Sara asked.

Hoitdle looked at Leitman, who for the first time took his gaze off us and looked back at Hoitdle.

Hoitdle looked at me and without saying a word, he walked over and took a seat opposite us.

"Doctor Hoitdle, is there something wrong?" Sara inquired.

"There has been a little problem with Eddie, I'm afraid to announce," Hoitdle said and bowed his head.

"What problem?" I interjected, worried.

"When you all got back, everything appeared to be fine. We put you back in your rooms to recover. Eddie was the first to come around. Maybe a bit too quick. But he awoke in a frenzy and started to attack our people and we could not control him, so Leitman here had to put him out. We tried to sedate him, but he was like a caged animal. He was foaming at the mouth, shouting all kinds of obscenities and ranting like a mad man and trying to attack me," Hoitdle said, then paused.

"What happened to him, is he okay now?" Sara asked with much more assertiveness.

"We had to unfortunately hit him over the head and knock him out. He is in isolation," Hoitdle replied.

"Jesus! Where?" I asked.

"We have a room down in the basement – it's a kind of holding-room for such incidents. He'll be okay, I'm sure of it," Hoitdle finished.

"I want to see him," Sara demanded.

Leitman spoke for the first time and said sternly, "You can't, he is still out of it and for security reasons, no one goes near him."

I looked to Doctor Hoitdle and asked, "Please Doctor, can't we see him just for a few moments?"

"It's out of my hands now, I'm afraid," he replied.

"I hope we are not going to have a problem with you too," Leitman said, staring right at me. Hoitdle starred at me too and waited to see how I would react. I looked at each one of them in turn and was about to protest when Sara jumped in.

"No, I'm sure it's for the best, and we can see him when he's feeling more like the Eddie we know."

Hoitdle looked at Sara and then me and said, "Good, it's settled then. Hermann, we won't be needing you now. You may go and do your security checks." With that, Leitman left the room, but not without giving me a look of contempt. He closed the sliding doors behind him, and straightaway the butler walked in, almost as if he knew he was needed to break the ice-cold atmosphere.

"Ah, the bubbly," Hoitdle said in a happy manner. The butler had three glasses already poured on a silver platter. He leaned towards Doctor Hoitdle and offered him a glass first. Hoitdle took up two and stood to hand one to both of us, before turning back to collect the third glass and saying, "A toast."

Sara and I looked at each other and slowly stood up.

"What shall we drink to?" Hoitdle asked us.

"How about to Eddie?" Sara said.

Hoitdle paused for a moment, and with a raised eyebrow said, "Sure – why not, yes. In fact, how about to Eddie, and to your safe return home?"

"To Eddie and humanity," I added.

With that we all repeated, "To Eddie and humanity." Hoitdle appeared to smirk at that right before taking a gulp of his expensive champagne. Sara took a small sip as did I and we sat back down.

"Now, we need to talk about the future – or the past," Hoitdle chuckled to himself. "Sara, with our good friend Eddie not feeling himself, as you put it, we will need to think of someone to accompany you back to document the other time periods we agreed upon. Have you anyone in mind?" he asked. Just as she was about to answer, he butted in, "Because I think in light of current situations, it might be better to send someone to oversee things, to ensure your safety. So, with that in mind, I'm thinking our resident head of security."

"Are you kidding? That buffoonish lump of meat? Er, no, thank you, I'd rather go on my own," she quipped.

I entered the conversation then. "Sara, you can't go alone. What if something happened to you? We'd never know."

"He's right," Hoitdle agreed.

"I was thinking maybe I could go with you, Sara," I said.

"No John, you don't need to do that," Sara replied, and placed her hand on my knee.

"You can't do that, Mr. Ryan, she's right; but not for any reason other than you are far too valuable to this whole operation. We need you here. We need your blood. If something was to go wrong while you both were back in the past, well, that would be that. Lost in that time, no way to jump, no fix. I can't allow it," he said in an angry tirade.

"It's my choice," I said firmly.

"John, look at me," Sara said calmly. I turned to see her face soften. She took both my hands in hers and said, "Your being alive here is what will keep me alive there. I need you to stay here to ensure my return. Can you do that for me, John?"

I let out a sigh, lowered my shoulders and replied, "For you, Sara; I would follow you to the ends of time, and I may just end up doing that. But yes, I'll stay and wait for you. For you." I emphasised those last two words. She smiled, leaned in and kissed me on the cheek.

Hoitdle stood up and raised his glass towards us and with little empathy said, "To you two," and downed his drink in one. "I will leave you two to talk. There is food prepared in the kitchen; please help yourselves, and we shall finalise the finer details in the morning. Till then, goodnight." He left the room and we were alone.

We got up and took up his offer of food as we were hungry and needed to eat. And eat we did. Bellies stuffed on fresh bread, meats, cooked chicken, large helpings of mixed salad and washed down with glasses of red wine. We were both feeling quite tired again as we adjusted to being home after a long and tiresome trip across time and space. When we had finished, we decided to get some sleep.

We left the kitchen and I walked Sara to her room. We stopped outside her room and I leaned in and kissed her goodnight. She asked me if I wanted to come in. I looked at her but a nagging thought kept going around in my mind; I told her there was something I needed to do, and I'd be back in a while. She nodded and went into her room and started to close her door.

I asked her to lock it behind her and waited until I heard the key turn before I walked across the hall back to my room and closed the door. I sat down on the bed, thinking about what could have happened to Eddie. I decided to wait till everyone was asleep and take a walk around the mansion. Even that goon Leitman must sleep sometime. I lay down and decided to go at two in the morning. As I lay there, I had an overwhelming gut feeling that something was just not right. Was Doctor Hoitdle telling us everything?

I knew he had an office downstairs, just off the main hall entrance. Maybe I could snoop around and see if I might find some answers; I really hoped I was wrong and that we would keep to our original plans and be done with it. I was also eager to see for myself the world outside of the mansion. The curiosity was almost overwhelming, and I had thoughts of running outside and not stopping until I saw what I needed to see. I was, after all, still in Germany, at the centre of it all. Did the world belong to the Nazis, and was there an acceptance of it? *All in good time*, I thought. Once Sara had jumped again, I would have another six months to see for myself and take in its ugly glory.

But for tonight, I would delve deeper into Hoitdle's affairs and see if I could find any revealing clues to any ulterior motives; and, maybe, finally lay my overwhelming guilt to rest.

As I checked my watch it read 01:47 and I decided to go now. I was restless and running out of patience. I got off the bed and headed to the door, keeping my shoes off. I opened the door slowly and took a peek outside, left and then right.

I could see no one. I left the room and walked to Sara's door. I listened closely and heard nothing. I made my way down the corridor to the stairs. I paused and listened again. Hearing nothing, I proceeded down until I reached the bottom and headed towards Hoitdle's office. I waited once more to listen for sounds and when I heard nothing I reached for the handle. I was pleasantly surprised to find it unlocked. I slowly pushed the door open, stepped inside and closed the door behind me. The room was quite large with rows and rows of shelves, holding hundreds of books, adorning the walls. On the centre wall to my right I heard the tick-tock of an old mahogany grandfather clock, with its brass pendulum and glass window. By the window stood a large oak desk which dominated the room with its bulky presence. It held a simple pen rest, some papers in a wooden tray and one thick empty glass on a silver coaster. There was a dusty, old-fashioned lamp to the right side of the desk, with a simple pull-chain to turn it on. I approached the desk in slow steps, still listening for movement outside the room. I rounded the desk and got to the window where lace curtains were drawn. I gently pulled one side back to peek outside and was startled by an armed guard strolling by. I recoiled and waited. After a few more moments I took another peek to find the guard had kept on patrolling the grounds.

I heaved a sigh and turned to the large desk. A leather swivel chair was in front and I pulled it back gently. There were three drawers on each side and one slim one in the centre at the opening of the table. I pulled that open first and only saw pens, ink and some paper clips. I sat on the chair and started to open each drawer trying to be as quiet as I could. It was hard to see in the darkness what was inside, even though my eyes had adjusted to the dark. I brought the lamp nearer the drawers and, taking a quick look outside and seeing no one, I pulled the chain and the light came on, dimly illuminating the room. I brought it down to the drawers to hide the light somewhat from the rest of the room. After looking in all six drawers I found nothing of interest or concern, except for a small metal key which I picked up in the bottom left drawer. *What could this be for?*

I took the lamp and pointed it around the room until I stopped it at a cabinet in the right-hand corner of the room. I got up and moved the lamp to the far side of the desk and onto the floor so not to be seen from outside. I pointed it towards the cabinet. I quietly moved towards the corner of the room. Stopping at the cabinet I placed the key into the single lock. I somehow knew it would open, and it did. I pulled open the top drawer of the two drawers and found a folder with hundreds of papers but, unable to make out the words, I brought it back to the lamp. I sat down on the floor and directed the lamplight onto the folder. It was untitled, and I opened the first page.

It had three simple indexed names. The first was *Ursprunglicher Plan*, meaning Initial Plan, the second—alarmingly—was *John Ryan*, and the third was *Eine Deutsche Welt*: A German World. My first thought was that this was probably Hoitdle's plans for what we had set out to achieve. The titles made sense, but I had to read more into it and see what it meant. The only problem was I didn't read that much German, and needed it translated. I had to take a risk; I had to take these to Sara. I locked the cabinet back up and put the lamp back in place on the desk. After one last look around I headed to the door and opened it slowly, pausing to listen for any noises. Hearing nothing, I came out and gently closed the door behind me. I made my way to the stairs and started back up. Just then, I heard the main front door start to open.

I ran up the rest of the stairs and just made it to the top when I heard German voices at the bottom. I peeked back around the corner of the stairs and saw two guards chatting and to my relief they had not noticed my presence on the stairs. One headed towards the kitchen as the other went back outside. I waited for both to disappear and made my way down the hall landing towards Sara's room. I got outside and looked back to check for anyone. Seeing and hearing nothing I tapped lightly on the door and tried to open the door. It was still locked; presumably Sara was in bed, asleep. I knocked a little harder, afraid someone might hear me. Then I heard movement inside the room. The door unlocked and Sara peeked out.

"What's going on?" she asked, still trying to adjust to the darkness

"It's okay. Sara, I found something," I said quickly.

"Come inside before someone sees you. What's that you've got?"

"Sorry for waking you, but I need to show you something – I need your help translating this," I said as I held out the folder from Hoitdle's study.

"What is this?" she asked.

"I found it in Doctor Hoitdle's study just now, and it has something to do with our project. I need to see if it has anything— I don't know, maybe something sinister about what we're doing," I explained.

"What the hell are you doing going through Hoitdle's personal stuff – are you trying to get yourself hurt or something?" she said in a worried voice.

"I need to be sure that what we are doing is exactly what Hoitdle said he would do. And if not, well, we need to put a stop to it," I said. She just looked at me in an inquisitive way and then at the folder. She brought it over to the bedside, turned on the lamp and opened the first page. I sat down on the edge of her bed and looked at how beautiful she looked, even after sleeping.

"There's a lot here, give me some time to read through it," she asked.

"Okay, I'll go back to my room, in case anyone comes looking for us. Come and find me when you're done."

She just nodded and said, "Okay, John, I will."

After looking in silence at each other for a few moments, I got up off the bed and headed back to my room, crossed the hallway to my door, went in and closed it behind me. I lay on the bed and closed my eyes. I tried hard to stay awake, but I knew Sara could be some time. After a few minutes I drifted off into a deep sleep.

"John, John – wake up, wake up, John!" I awoke to the sound of Sara's voice and her shaking my arms as she woke me.

"What's up? Is everything okay," I asked.

"You were right," she said.

"Right about what?"

"About Hoitdle, he's not what he claims to be."

"What do you mean?"

"I've read it through, the first two parts in here are all in order, as far as I can tell. The 'Initial Plan' is about going back to the past, and all the files on us and, of course, BETI. The file with your name is about your life, your past, your family history, medical records – nothing sinister, nothing you didn't already know. But the third part is…well, it's all a lie. All of it."

"Explain what you mean," I demanded to know, now alert and fully awake as I waited to hear the worst.

"It starts out just like we agreed, documenting the changes in time. But when it's all done, when we have all done our little part of the plan, Hoitdle and his team plan to leave it that way. No going back to return the past to the past. They want a new world order, just as Hitler had planned but failed. When we allow Germany to win the war and we come back to our present time, Hoitdle plans to destroy BETI, so nothing can be returned to its original history. He wants the Nazi state as Hitler had always dreamed of. And he'll get it," Sara said, with tears in her eyes. "What have we done, John?"

"It's not too late, if we can stop him," I said, reaching out my hand to her face.

"There is one more thing I found out about Hoitdle," she said.

"What is it?" I asked.

"Look at his name, John, look very closely at his name," she said looking at me intently. As I looked down at a sheet of paper with his name on it from the file, I didn't see it at first. Ralf Hoitdle. It looked familiar, but what was I not seeing? As Sara took a pen and circled the A, then the D and then the O from his name, I then saw it; the rest of the name became apparent.

I looked up at Sara and called it out. "Adolf Hitler…"

She fell into my arms and I held her tight. I didn't want to let go. I pulled her back and looked into her eyes. Doctor Hoitdle was a cover name. He was using an anagram of Hitler's name as some kind of tribute to the man he really adored.

"So, who the hell is Ralf Hoitdle?" I said.

"That is what we need to find out," Sara said.

"We're not going to let him get away with it, but we need help," I said.

She nodded in agreement and asked, "Who can help us here?"

"Only one man can help us, but he doesn't know it yet," I replied.

"Who?" she asked.

"Hoitdle. We need to play along for now, and find a way to get him to send us back to 1941, find the original machine and destroy it," I said.

"But if we do that, John, how would we get back home after?" she asked. I just looked at her and she recoiled back. She knew what I was saying. We would be stuck in the past, but it was what we had to do. Two people from 2003 living in the past would be better than the alternative, Hoitdle and his followers changing the future forever; a Nazi future would be just too much to bear. We had helped bring this madness to life, and we were going to fix it.

"Okay John; let's do this, but let's do it together, all the way to back to 1941," Sara said, holding onto both of my shaking hands. I squeezed hers in return and repeated her words. "Let's do this."

Chapter 16
Lost Friends

WE GATHERED UP THE STOLEN file and planned to return it to Hoitdle's study before he found out it was missing. Sara got herself dressed and I waited by the door to listen for any unwanted attention. "I'm ready," she said. I just nodded and gestured to her. We made our way out of the bedroom and down the hallway. We stopped at the top of the staircase and listened again. Hearing nothing, we headed down and reached the bottom. Turning right and around the staircase we made our way to the study. Sara opened the door and peaked inside.

"Okay," she said. I followed her inside and closed the door. "Where was it?" she asked. I went over to the large wooden desk and opened the bottom drawer which held the key to the cabinet. I took it out and went over to the cabinet to unlock it. Sara handed me the file and I placed it back as I found it. I locked it again and retuned to place the key back in the drawer. I nodded in triumph to Sara and we both headed to the door. I opened it slightly and checked outside. It appeared normal. We both moved outside and closed the door behind us. As we made our way towards the stairs, we were stopped in our tracks as we heard his voice.

"Good evening, my worldly travellers." Hoitdle's distinguished voice travelled across the hall foyer. We turned around and saw him there. "Why don't you two join me in the next room?" he said, gesturing us over. We looked at each other. We looked at the front door, and one thought ran through my mind: even without my shoes on, I wanted to run out with Sara in tow.

Taking a few steps towards Hoitdle and about to make a move, from the far right of the foyer and out of the shadows, Leitman stepped out of the darkness into the dim light. We could see he held in his hand a pistol of some sort, and he just stood there waiting for a command with a wry smile on his face. Having no real choice, we slowly made our way into the other room as ordered.

Hoitdle let us go in first, and there we found his other cohorts standing around waiting for us to join them. "Please, sit down, everyone, please," Hoitdle said as he waved his hand around in a circle to include everyone in the room. We were joined by Doctor Grundle, our surgeon, and Marko Hinterberg, our communications and electronics expert. Leitman rolled in behind Hoitdle, came to one side and held his gaze on Sara and I, while tapping his weapon against his leg as if to remind us it was there. We all sat down and waited for Hoitdle to do the same. He eventually sat down after pouring himself a drink from a drinks trolley by his side.

"It appears we are in a bit of a predicament, aren't we?" he said, looking at Sara and then me.

"What do you mean?" I asked nervously.

"Oh, come now, Mr. Ryan, let's not play these silly games now, shall we?" Hoitdle said raising his thin eyebrows. I looked at Sara and then turned to Hoitdle and I knew I had to play along.

"Okay, Doctor Hoitdle; we know why we're really here, and what your true plans are. We've both seen your file, from your study. The third part especially triggered my interest," I said.

"Oh, is that right, John? Well, you see, I already knew that. We have our ways of knowing pretty much everything that goes on around here," he said in a jovial way.

I once more looked at Sara and made my move. "It's okay, Doctor Hoitdle, we want in. We believe in this project now; we want to see it all the way to the end. It's too important to stop now. We will do whatever it takes to help you and your people to make this happen, you can trust us," I said, trying to sound convincing.

He looked around the room at Hinterberg and Grundle and then simultaneously they all burst out laughing.

Sara piped up. "What's so funny, Doctor Hoitdle?"

"You, Sara, and you, John, that is what is so funny," he replied. "You see, Marko here, our communications expert— well, I'll let him explain what he is also good at."

Looking at Hinterberg, we listened. "It's not just BETI that I am here to work on, my two little snoopers, I am here to ensure that no one betrays our project. With that in mind this whole mansion is wired for sound, cameras and motion detectors. We see and hear everything, including you two fools," he said and leaned back, looking smug. Sara looked at me and sank back into her seat.

"Okay, Doctor Hoitdle, you seem to be holding all the cards. Or should I say, Adolf Hitler? A little unoriginal, I might add. So what now?"

He leaned back and, looking a little put out with my comment, he took a sip of whiskey from his glass then stood up. "Well, Mr. Ryan, for us, we get to complete our plans and you will help us achieve that with that blood of yours; so for now, you belong to us until we decide you are no longer useful," he said, so matter-of-fact.

"And what about me, Doctor Hoitdle, what happens to me?" Sara said. I looked at Hoitdle and waited for a response. He looked around at our not-so-friendly guard and said, "Our good friend Leitman here will take very good care of you, my dear Sara."

"Wait a minute!" I said, standing up to protest.

"Sit down," Hoitdle shouted sternly at me.

"Sara has done nothing to you, and in fact has carried out all her instructions to the letter," I pleaded with Hoitdle. With that, Leitman took four steps forward, pointed the gun at my head and with his gun gestured to me to sit back down. Everyone stared at me and waited for my actions. I stared back at the barrel of the gun for a few moments and could see the trigger being clicked. I felt a hand on my arm. It was Sara pulling me back and her eyes were telling me to sit back down. I looked at her and followed her gaze and sat down.

"Good, you made the right decision, Mr. Ryan," Hoitdle said, and with that got up and left the room. Hinterberg and Grundle also stood, and said something to Leitman in German.

"Get up and come with me," Leitman said in his strong German accent, pointing the gun in Sara's direction. She got up, looked at me, then suddenly leaned in and kissed me on the lips.

"Take care, John," she said and went to move.

I pulled her back and whispered, "It's not over, I'll find you. I'll find a way." She just smiled, pulled away and turned to walk out with Leitman who led her out of the room and out the front door of the foyer. I heard the door close behind them and my heart sank.

"You have to come with us," Hinterberg said.

"And don't try anything, Ryan, as Leitman is not the only one carrying protection," Grundle said while pulling out a handgun from his jacket pocket.

I looked at him and asked, "Where are we going?"

"Where do you think?" he replied.

Once again, we were making our way back to see BETI and to an unknown destination. As we got to the button control to enter the door to BETI, I jumped in rigid fright, as I heard a single gun shot from outside the mansion. "No, Sara," I said to myself and bowed my head. I felt an anger coming over me and turned to the two men. Grundle, still pointing the gun at me, ordered me inside with a simple statement.

"Keep moving. There is nothing you can do for your pretty girlfriend anymore."

With a heavy heart I proceeded inside and thought of giving up. *Should I just let them shoot me?* At least my nightmare would be over and I would maybe see my dad again. I envisaged him waiting for me with his big smile, asking in a sarcastic voice, *"Boy, what the hell did you do?"* but holding out his arms to welcome me home. I also thought of my friends, my family, the whole world, and of Sara. Was she really dead? I had to try to fix what I had done. I was just yet to figure out how I would do that, or if it would be possible to do it on my own.

I headed towards the chamber of horrors, sat on a chair and as I put my head in my hands, I felt the sadness of what had just happened escalating to new levels. I saw it in her eyes as she left the room, the pain and the sorrow and it was tearing me up inside. I promised myself in those moments to put things right, and if I had to do it alone, then that's what I would do.

I had never felt so alone as I did in that moment.

As I slowly came around from my moments of sadness, I saw Hoitdle was already in the room and had begun the process of preparing BETI for my next jump.

"It was quite a regrettable business, but unfortunately out of my hands, John," Hoitdle said calmly.

"Fuck you," was all I could muster.

With a drop of his mouth and a stupid smile, he returned to what he was doing as Grundle ordered me up. I turned my head and gave him a look that said *I'm going to kill you soon.* Grundle just smirked and held his gun pointed in my direction. Hinterberg locked the door to the room.

I looked over at Hoitdle.

"So, who are you really? When we met in 1943, you were still Hoitdle. When did you assume that name, and why?" I asked.

"All very good questions, Mr. Ryan, and I will answer them all, but first, please, if you will," Hoitdle said and pointing towards the gurney on the right of the room with a needle laid out on the tray. I slowly walked over and Grundle followed, keeping enough distance to avoid a confrontation. I sat up on it and rolled up my sleeve. Grundle passed the gun to Hinterberg and walked to my side. He tapped his fingers on a vein in my right arm and took up the needle. Taking a glance at me he pushed the needle into my vein and slowly withdrew a vial of blood.

"We'll need more of that," Hoitdle said as I saw Grundle smiling to himself. Grundle put a swab over the spot where the vein had been raided and folded my arm up, almost showing care.

"So, you were about to tell me who you really are…" I asked again.

"Okay, John, I guess you deserve to know the whole truth after everything we've been through together," he said, as if we were buddies who just endured a battle on the front.

And so, he began to tell his story and I sat in silence and listened.

"It was November 9, 1938; that date will probably ring a bell with you, the night of Kristallnacht. You know, the night all Jewish businesses and homes were looted and ransacked. Well, I was a relatively-unknown scientist trying to make my way from college graduate to respected science researcher in the Kaiser Wilhelm Society of Berlin, an institution founded by another Adolf, Adolf Harnack in 1911. I was on my way home when as I walked past a dark lane way, I noticed two men kicking and beating another older gentleman. So, I ran to help him, and his two assailants ran off.

"The man was in a bad way, so I picked him up and took him to my apartment to clean him up. I had asked the gentleman what they were beating him for. It turns out they were two young Jewish men, getting revenge on any German they came across for their father's leather shop getting ransacked on that crazy night of the broken glass. It meant nothing to me, you see," Hoitdle said. "They were the times we were living in. As I cleaned up his wounds, we started talking. I asked him his name and what he did. He told me his name was Karl Schmied. He was a physicist working for the Nazis at a weapon-manufacturing facility. He was very grateful to me for saving him from further injury, and once he found out that I too was a budding young scientist, there was an immediate connection and we ended up talking for hours. He then asked me if I'd like to come assist him at one of their facilities. I was of course so excited I immediately jumped at the offer. Maybe this was my chance to make something of myself, I thought. So that's where it all started for me. The following week, I was given new papers and told to make my way by train to the town of Hillersleben, Germany. It was a weapons research centre. A sprawling facility in the forested hills. Heavily guarded, it was to become my home for the next few months and while there, I was bunked in with a certain John Joseph Ryan."

"My grandfather," I said.

"Yes, John," Hoitdle said. He continued. "We became quite close, eating, working and bunking together. At first, they had us working on rocket manufacturing and the like. It was wartime after all, but we were learning so much and I also had the support of my new tutor and now friend, Doctor Karl Schmied, who in all fairness had ensured we got the best of everything: food, drink, and the occasional woman. Ha," he chuckled to himself. "One day, Doctor Schmied came to our sleeping quarters and shut the door. He said he was working on a new project. One of very high importance, and one that could ensure Germany's victory over the Allies and protect the one thousand-year Reich. He asked if we wanted to come and help him achieve this.

"I of course didn't hesitate and said yes. Your grandfather, still the reluctant scientist in a Nazi regime, eventually agreed after much cajoling from me. You may have heard rumours of a Solar Death Ray the Nazis were working on. It was based on the original designs of physicist Hermann Oberth and in 1929 he wrote a book called *Wege Zur Raumschiffahrt* or 'Ways to Spaceflight'. In it he talked about the first manned spaceflight and its possibilities. Of course, he wanted to build a space facility that could harness the sun for earth to use as an energy source. But the military had other ideas and were excited by its weapons capabilities.

"With another scientist, Wernher Von Braun ,who you know designed the V2 rocket, along with me, your grandfather, Schmied and a few other engineers were tasked with using this new technology and ideas and coming up with a powerful weapon that could be used against Allied aircraft to knock them out of the skies. And this, my friend, is where we discovered BETI. We were given orders to change our identities for utter secrecy, and so began our project. I suppose picking Hitler's name as an anagram was a little hysterical of me, but I was young, impressionable and still a bit idealistic, and your grandfather thought it was silly but quite amusing. And this is where we, by accident, discovered something even more destructive than a death ray, a time machine. Your grandfather—as you now know—engineered a secret bio code to keep the Nazis from taking total control of the weapon. In those early stages, he didn't really know what we had and could not afford to allow Hitler's henchmen to take it away before we could test it in the right controlled manner. After the first test was successful your grandfather engineered a code to prevent the Nazis using it without our control. This part of the code was what we were missing all this time, until we found out about it right before your Grandfather's death. Later on, we thought we could get it to work with any blood, overcome that part of it, but it would never work. And so, it led us all the way to you, Mr. Ryan." Hoitdle finally concluded his story.

"So why are we here now?" I asked.

"We are going to stockpile your blood, Mr. Ryan, keep just enough to finish this project and then put BETI away. Keep her away from any other government or foreign agency that ever comes to destroy or take her away from us. She will never be found again. Not unless I decide. If I die, she will die with me," he said.

"And what of me? You know, when you've bled me dry and have no more use for me, what happens to me then?" I asked.

"You know, Mr. Ryan, I've been asking myself that question for the last while now, and I haven't decided. I've become quite fond of you, John. You remind me very much of your grandfather," Hoitdle replied.

Sitting there, I began trying to work out distractions, so I could escape. But what would I be escaping to? What kind of world was out there? What did Europe now look like, and particularly what did home look like? Would I see my family and friends again? Would I witness the swastika flying over the General Post Office in my beloved Dublin, rebuilt from the destruction of the 1916 Easter Rising only to end up here?

Hoitdle spoke, "Okay, Mr. Ryan, we need you to step into BETI now. You are going to go back to 1975. We want you to document and film for three months and bring it back to us,"

"And if I refuse?" I asked.

Hinterberg interjected. "Ryan, just remember we know everything about you – especially your family back home, Mamma and Sister."

"Son of a bitch, if you touch any of my family, I will fucking kill you," I shouted at him.

"Oh, come now, Mr. Ryan, no need for any of that – because you are going to do as we say, aren't you?" Hoitdle said with unbearable smugness.

Knowing these people, I knew I didn't have a choice, and agreed to go if they agreed to one condition.

"What is that?" Hoitdle asked.

"Sara," I said. "Will you change that when I come back? Will you agree to go back in time, to just before you had her shot by your goon, and let her go? Do that for me, and I will fully cooperate and give you what you want willingly," I pleaded.

Hoitdle looked at his henchmen, Hinterberg and Grundle, and then turned to me, nodded his head and said, "Why not? We will do that for you, Mr. Ryan. If the girl makes you a happier participant, then it is agreed."

Just then Leitman entered the room and looked at me with his usual arrogance and smug face and I felt like I could run at him right now and pound his head into the wall. I decided to wait and turned my head back to Hoitdle's direction.

Not really trusting a word out of Hoitdle's mouth, I just nodded back and stood up.

"Everything you need is already inside the dome; camera design from the seventies. Security won't be as tight as it was in 1941, with the war being over for nearly thirty years, but you may still come across state secret police so we have given you new identity papers and a weapon. Your destination will be London. We want to see what a defeated country looks like from the point of view from our biggest threat at the start of the war. We assume we will have occupying troops and Gestapo there, so you still need to be very careful. But being Irish and speaking perfect English, you should be able to blend in much better this time, and know your way around a little better, don't you think, Mr. Ryan?" Hoitdle concluded.

"I assume so," I said with little enthusiasm.

"Come now, try to be more upbeat than that," he said.

"Let's just get on with this charade," I demanded.

"Okay, everyone, let's take our places and begin our next countdown," Hoitdle ordered everyone. Grundle and Hinterberg took up their positions. Leitman was ordered to check the mansion grounds to ensure no one was around and Hoitdle locked the door after him. My eyes followed him right out the door as I had murderous thoughts invade my mind.

And then it came to me: the weapon in the dome. That was going to be my chance. I would have to wait until the dome door closed over, grab the weapon from the box, load it and shoot at the panels to try stop the process.

I wasn't sure if it would even work. I wasn't sure if it would kill me. Could it explode? Would I be transported into space, or obliterated? But I had to try something. I knew I was risking damaging the machine, which would leave me unable to get back to 1941 at some stage to repair the harm we had caused, but it was a chance I had to take in order to get out of here. I could get help and come back with the right people to fix what we had done. Surely, with the right people we could come back, take the machine from Hoitdle and redeem our shameful actions?

"Okay, Ryan, it's time for you to take another step through time. Please enter and take your place," Hoitdle said, while pointing his hand towards BETI.

I took one last look around at their positions and made my way towards the entry point. Looking at Hoitdle, I turned and stepped inside.

"See you in three months," Hoitdle said.

As the door started to close, I glanced down at the metal cases that had been placed inside. The door closed and I heard it seal. I quickly open the first case and then the next. I found the gun along with a box of shells. I quickly loaded the gun and looked around at the panels in the dome. The start-up had begun. I envisaged the three men outside going through the sequencing to countdown.

I knew my best chance would be when the noise levels were at their highest, when they might not hear the shot and if BETI stopped working, they may think it was an error they had made.

And so, it began, the aircraft like-noise of the dome started increasing with every circulating flash. I had to ensure I shot at just the right time. I could not afford to pass out. I waited and waited. My brain began to hurt, and my ears were at deafening levels, and I started to feel dizzy. I took my chance. At the door-locking mechanism, I noticed a tiny red light that was most likely some sort of magnetic lock. I aimed the gun towards this point and held it as steady as I could. Just as I felt I was about to pass out, I took the shot. I fell to my knees. Head bowed down, I dropped the gun and covered my ears and waited to pass out before being transported back in time.

Then, just as I thought I was blacking out, the noise levels started to decrease. The flashing started to slow, and I started to come around a little. Gathering any energy I had, I felt around for the gun. My hand reached it, but my eyes were still a little blurry. I didn't know if Hoitdle and the others knew what I had done, so I thought my best plan was to play dead; lay still on my side with my gun hidden under me, wait for the doors to open and then take my chance. It seemed like fifteen minutes had passed before I heard it. The door hissed a little and opened only slightly. I could hear Hoitdle say something but could not quite make it out. After a few more muffled sounds, I began to make sense of it. "Ryan, Ryan, are you okay in there?" Hoitdle was shouting into the machine.

I believed I may have gotten away with it. Maybe they just didn't know what I had done. Laying very still I waited to see if my plan came to fruition. Again, the door hissed some more as they struggled to open BETI. I could hear all four men now trying to wedge the door open. I must have damaged the automatic opening system. A few moments later I heard the door give way. Hoitdle stepped in and crouched down beside me as I faced away from him on my side. Grundle and Hinterberg were standing just at the entrance of the dome and waited to find out my condition.

"Is he alive?" Grundle asked of Hoitdle. Just as Hoitdle put his hand on my shoulder, I rolled over slowly pretending to just come out of consciousness and bringing my hand around I pointed the gun into his stomach.

Looking down at what had just stuck in his belly, his eyes quickly turned to meet mine and he smiled. "Bravo, Mr. Ryan," he said. I pushed him back and got up quickly before the others could react.

Hinterberg went to reach for his gun and I pointed the gun at him and said, "Don't move a muscle." He didn't look compliant. His hand moved towards his pocket and I shot him, hitting him in the shoulder. He fell back as Hoitdle and Grundle looked shocked, and watched Hinterberg fall to the ground. They turned back to me and put their hands out, as if to say *don't shoot*. I ordered them to step back away from me. I got up from the surface of the dome and waved them back out into the centre of the room.

They stepped back, all the while keeping eye contact, and I ordered them to stop and drop to their knees.

Hinterberg was still alive but lay groaning on the ground with a bullet lodged in his left shoulder and bleeding heavily.

"You surprised me, Mr. Ryan," Hoitdle said with a smirk on his face.

"I surprised myself," I smirked back.

"Now what?" Hoitdle asked.

"Now, I get the fuck out of here," I said.

"And go where? You are in a different dimension now, John, with nowhere to turn. Why don't you put the gun down and we can all talk this through?" Hoitdle said?

"Yeah, sure, and we'll all just forget this ever happened, right?" I said sarcastically.

"You won't get very far, Ryan." Words coming from Grundle.

"Maybe I won't, but neither will you, you fat fuck," I replied, and with that I pointed the gun at his head and pulled the trigger and he fell sideways to the ground as dark red blood started pouring from the hole in his head. As the smoke from the gun rose into the air, I looked at Hoitdle and he stared back, in shock at what he had thought I was incapable of. I could hardly believe it myself. I felt an overwhelming feeling come over me and I could not stop. I turned to the groaning Hinterberg and once again pointed the gun at his head.

"Don't do it, Ryan," I heard Hoitdle scream. I ignored his pleas and as Hinterberg looked up in fear he begged, "No, no," and reached out his hand to stop the bullet. I blew the injured man's head off. His head dropped back down and to the side and he lay still.

I turned to Hoitdle and he looked forlornly resigned to his fate.

As I pointed the gun at his head, I thought of my family back home. I thought of Eddie and Sara.

How would I get back home? Would I even have a home? Germany had won the war – what had it done to Ireland?

Something inside of me could not bring me to pull the trigger. At the back of my mind, I had the thought that just maybe, there was a way to change all this; a way to right the wrongs of what we all had done here at the mansion. And, worst of all, I knew that if it anything was going to change; I would need this monster to help me change it back.

Suddenly I heard banging on the door. It was Leitman. He must have heard the shots.

"Open up! What's going on in there? Doctor Hoitdle, are you okay?"

"Not a word," I said quietly to Hoitdle, as I pointed the gun in his direction once more. "Get up," I instructed Hoitdle, and waved him to the door. As he got to the door, I ordered Hoitdle to tell Leitman, "Everything is okay, and you are going to open the door." He complied and as he did, I stood to the right side of the door and waited for it to open. Once the click of the lock opened, I waved Hoitdle to step back. The door pushed open and Leitman took four steps in. He instantly stopped in his tracks and stared at Hoitdle, for he now felt my gun at the back of his head.

"Drop it," I said. Leitman looked at Hoitdle as if waiting for instructions and Hoitdle nodded his approval and Leitman dropped his gun like a well-trained soldier. I lifted the butt of my gun up and struck Leitman with all my might on the back of his head and he slumped in a heap unconscious to the floor.

"Tie him up," I ordered Hoitdle. He complied, using cable ties from a drawer in a desk in the dome chamber. I told Hoitdle to put his hands behind his back and tied them together. Then I sat him down beside a pipe running down the wall in the far-left corner of the room and used more cable ties to tie him to that. I also tied his feet.

I stood up and looked down at Doctor Hoitdle for I did not know if I would ever cross paths with him again.

"Good luck, John. I hope you find what you're looking for," Hoitdle said, almost sounding caring.

Saying nothing in return, I took a quick look around and made my way quickly out of the door and closed it behind me and headed up the spiral staircase. I headed straight for the main door, As I was nearing the door, Nurse Muller appeared at the bottom of the stairs holding a tray with some medical instruments and little paper cups for taking pills. I pointed the gun in her direction.

"Don't shoot me, please," she begged.

"Step down from the stairs and place the tray on the ground," I ordered her. She immediately obeyed and raised her hands in the air. "What happened with Eddie?"

"I, I, I'm not sure," she stuttered.

"Okay, I'm going to ask you one more time, and this time, if you lie to me again, you will be the third person to die by this gun today. Where is Eddie?" I demanded to know.

"I don't know what exactly happened. But I saw Leitman and another guard dragging what looked like a body wrapped in sheets up from the holding cell and out to the garden space, about two hours before you and Sara were brought around," she said finally.

"Are you sure it was Eddie?" I asked.

"I don't know who else it could be, and that man scares me, so I don't like to ask questions around here," she replied with a quiver in her voice.

"You mean Leitman," I said. She just nodded. "Yeah, he kind of scares me too," I said in return.

"You should go, just get out of here while you still can. The guards are not here at the moment, but they could be back at any minute," she said. Looking at her and feeling she was no threat to me, I put the gun away and backed off to the door. I opened it and quickly ran out into the open and down the driveway. I wanted to be sure about Eddie, but my gut was telling me the frightened nurse was telling the truth, and he had indeed been murdered by Leitman under Hoitdle's instructions. Fearing running into the guards, I ran as fast as I could and didn't look back. I was finally out of the mansion. Running past the open gates, down the quiet driveway and onto the tree-laden roads I first came to when I arrived at the mansion. I kept running until I could run no more and then I walked and walked hard and kept moving for what felt like a marathon. Before I even realised it, I became aware that it was beginning to become light. Dawn was breaking and I then began to wonder how the hell was I going to get out of Germany and back home. I walked some more and eventually came to the outskirts of a small town. I hide in a nearby treeline and waited until I could see people coming and going and then, I made my move to blend into the new world and find a way home.

Chapter 17
The New World

As I looked on across the fields from the treeline into the town, I could see a shop opening its doors. And there it was, flying proud over the awning: the red and black of the swastika flag. Other businesses had started to open, and I could see more people started to go this way and that. And then it struck me. No soldiers on the street. Why would there be? The war was long over, and Germany had won, life had moved on and this was just a way of life for them. Maybe I wouldn't look out of place. Did I have a choice? I left the treeline and made my way onto the narrow road towards the town. As I passed a woman in her forties, she just nodded at me and kept moving. I nodded back but said nothing. More people passed me, and no one took any notice. This was their normal. I was just another person on the street.

As I moved on down the town looking for something that could help me, I was astonished to hear American accents from two teen girls, in bohemian clothing and backpacks, walking towards me.

"Hey," one of them said smiling at me.

"Hey," I said back. I watched them walk past me. "Stop, wait," I called after them. They turned and stopped.

"Yeah, can we help you?"

Having a quick look around I asked, "Um, did you guys get here by bus, or a train maybe?"

"Yeah dude, there's a train station about two miles past that school building," Said the girl who had just smiled at me as she pointed down the street.

"Did you have any problems getting into Germany?" I asked them.

"No, why would we?" they replied.

"No reason. And thank you," I replied, and waved them on.

"No problem, bye," they both said and turned and went on about their exploring.

Just as I thought might have happened. Relations after the war would eventually heal and time would move on.

I had to see for myself, so I kept on moving and finally made my way to the train station. I was still in high alert mode and was constantly looking around waiting to see Hoitdle or Leitman. The train station was busy enough and I walked over to the ticket booth. I could hear German, English and French accents all around me.

Arriving at the ticket booth I asked for a ticket to Berlin with a connecting ticket to Paris. With no questions asked, and my English clearly understood, I was given the ticket as if in any European train station. It was as if they were used to travellers here all the time and nothing was unusual for them. It was surreal. I took my ticket and waited on a seat by platform three. It would be another twenty minutes for the train to arrive and I sat back, and people-watched. I could not believe how normal everything was. No Nazi soldiers, no state police questioning everyone. The only thing that was unusual was the presence of many swastika flags, flying over every building I came across including the train station. Maybe things would be okay after all.

I was excited, and nervous, too, about getting home.

Twenty minutes later, with German precision the train pulled up right on time and I boarded.

I took my seat and watched the sky as the train pulled away on the tracks towards Berlin. I felt drained and fell asleep for hours as the train pushed on to Berlin.

I awoke to the sound of people dislodging bags and cases from overhead racks just before the train arrived in Berlin. Looking around again I found no one checking me out or staring at me weirdly.

Once the train had stopped, I disembarked with the other passengers and made my way to the connecting platform and waited for the Paris inter-rail to bring me closer to home. I did not leave the station so I could not fully see how Berlin had changed, but for what I could observe, the buildings in the distance seemed to be structurally larger. I remember Hitler's grand plans to build megastructures in Berlin designed by Albert Speer, Germany's Minister of Armaments and War Production. He wanted Berlin to be adorned just like in the days of the Roman Empire.

I boarded the train and this time I did not sleep on the eight-and-a-half-hour journey. My brain was overloaded with all the changes I had seen. The larger the town or city, the more swastika flags were flying. I knew there was so much to see and to take in, but all I wanted to do now was get home. I could find everything I needed to know and see once I was home in Dublin again. I needed to see the people I loved once more, recoup and heal.

And then I could decide what I was going to do about Hoitdle and the New World.

Reaching Paris, I got off the train and immediately made my way to the airport by cab. My taxi driver looked at me, puzzled, as I called out the airport name. It was not called Charles De Gaulle airport now; it was called Goebbels International. It was only when I had reached the airport that I stupidly realised I had no passport to get home. I had to try another way. So I once again was on the road; this time, by bus to Cherbourg where I would try stowing away to get me to Ireland. Upon arrival I went to a café near the docks where I noticed many truckers filling up their bellies. I had to try to get on one of their vehicles. I waited for drivers to leave and followed them until I found one that I could get on. Once I picked my carrier, I got under an Irish truck labelled *Murphy's Transport Services*. I held onto the undercarriage and prayed I would not be found by local customs officers.

The truck pulled away with me underneath and headed towards the customs check point. The officers there checked the driver's passport and to my good fortune waved him through with no further checks. The truck arrived at an Irish Ferries ship, and drove on board.

It was directed to a holding point and stopped. I dropped to the floor and waited underneath. I waited until every vehicle was aboard and I heard the large cargo bay doors close. I then casually walked over to the stairs leading to the upper passenger levels and took a seat by the window. With a sigh of relief, I waited for the ship to sail away out of France. And sail it did, all the way to Rosslare. I was not the best sailor and felt sick at many points. I did not know if that was the movement of the sea or how I was feeling about everything that had happened. But either way I found myself up on the outer decks grabbing any fresh air I could until it eased.

It was such a relief when the ship finally docked at port.

I got off the boat at Rosslare and managed to blag a taxi-share with another guy to the train station. It was so strange seeing swastikas and tri-colours side by side all over the streets. I located the train for Dublin and had to try avoiding ticket inspectors as I had no money left on me.

I had hoped that this would finally be the last leg of my tiring journey home. The people on the train were mainly Irish, with a few foreign nationals, but looking out the window I witnessed many Nazi symbols. It was indeed a curious journey back to Dublin.

Eventually the train pulled in and I got off in Heuston Station in Dublin City.

It's nice to see this name hasn't changed, I thought.

I walked along the quays of the river Liffey and was feeling so happy to be back on Dublin soil, I felt a tear roll down my face. I passed the Four Courts and it was there that, to my utter contempt, I saw the first real evidence: a police car rolled by, but it did not have the Garda logo on the side. It had a swastika, and said *State Police*. The country was under Nazi rule. I saw more and more cars like this along with foot patrols with the same police symbols on their arms.

I tried to avoid eye contact with them and walked all the way to O'Connell Street. The street names appeared to be the same but there was something different, I noticed further down the middle of the street. And there it was. Bold as brass. There stood about forty feet high, a cast iron statue of Adolf Hitler. It had happened. He had conquered Europe. I saw a familiar bookstore I knew and headed for Eason's. I ran over the street to go inside. I headed straight for their history section on the ground floor at the back of the shop. *My God*, I thought. There were so many books on Germany and Hitler. I walked closer to the lined shelves and traced my eyes over the book covers. Stopping at one for no particular reason, other than the cover caught my eye. I picked it up and there on the cover I shook my head as I saw the incredible picture of the Pope locked in handshake with Adolf Hitler on the steps of the Vatican. '*A man of peace*', it was called, and I scoffed to myself at how terrible history can really be portrayed. Writers gloss over awful atrocities when they write about victors.

I opened it up and with the many pictures adorning its glossy pages, I began to read random sections.

One chapter was called '*How Hitler brought peace and posterity to Europe*'. It was surreal. In another it had Hitler in a picture with the Pope, dated 17th of August 1953, talking about how he wished for an end to all terror across the world. I was amazed but not surprised at how we can easily move on from such a frightening monster who conquered the world. Hitler had become the modern-day Alexander the Great and now he was cast as a brilliant leader, who fought the allies and won. He made peace with them over the years, under puppet governments of course, but the war had ended, and Germany was now the world leader of economics, architecture, politics and a military superpower with nuclear technology.

The final chapter was 'Long live the Führer'; he had died on 5th February 1967. Winning the war and having the best medical doctors around him, I guess he was able to live longer than he would have done with his original condition at the end of the war when he was a broken man. The Third Reich lived. It was 2003 and Germany was a celebrated country with pride, and one it appeared everyone wanted to now suck up to.

After the war, in my known world of 1945, America, the United Kingdom and Russia were the new superpowers, but not now. The British had lost the war and now answered to Germany. Both swastika and English flags flew in London and all across the United Kingdom.

I wondered what the British powers felt like, being ruled by a foreign power. They now knew how it felt after their many years of colonialism. I started flicking through other books and read that Germany was a nuclear power, and had vetoed all other European countries, including Russia, from having nuclear technologies.

The United States had pulled out of the war against the Axis powers early on, unable to get a foothold in France, and had decided they were not ready or able to face up against Germany and Japan at the same time. It would end up crippling their economy for decades to come.

It appeared that they fought Japan on their own and without the atom bombs they were supposed to have developed and dropped on Hiroshima and Nagasaki in 1945, the war against mainland Japan was halted and they signed a truce to end the war in the Pacific.

England, France and their other allies were left to their fate, as Germany held firm in Europe and with only having to fight on one front against Russia, they were able to hold them off and eventually push across its expanse and defeat them. They had the whole of Europe, Scandinavia and the Baltic states along with North Africa to call upon for food resources, oil, iron ore and manpower to crush the crumbling Russian juggernaut.

Placing one book back and taking another, it went on and on. Book after book. Germany had done it.

And then I saw it. I looked at one book sitting at the very end of the top right shelf. A deep shame came across me as I pulled it down and read its title: *The Holocaust and the Great Jewish Lie.* And there it was – 'An exaggerated rumour by surviving Jewish Europeans, to discredit the Germans.' The Nazis wrote about how Jewish settlers had moved east to join with Russia to fight against Germany and its other allies, Italy, Romania and Hungary. And after their defeat and camp internment, they made-up stories of genocide and SS death camps. Stories of hundreds of thousands of men, women and children every week being marched into Polish and German work camps and then being exterminated en masse. A great lie, the Germans wrote, and one they proved with visits to their territories over the years. Of course, by then the Nazis were able to cover it all up. There were no American or Russian forces arriving to free the camps. No evidence of those horrific black-and-white pictures of skeletons in striped pyjamas slowly coming out of their sleeping quarters; haggard, beaten, and broken shells of human torture. No evidence of mass burning and burial sites.

No Auschwitz-Birkenau, no Sobibor, and no Treblinka. Germany would have covered it all up. No aerial shots from Allied planes, as the Luftwaffe had ruled the skies. The systematic killing of the Jewish population was almost total, apart from the few that managed to escape to Russia and hide under new identities or the few who survived the death camps and moved to labour camps once the war was won. In reading books from the past, we know that over six million Jews were wiped out. It had to be more in this new world, as there was no one to stop the horrors and yet, because the Nazis won the war, time had moved on and the world had accepted the way it was. The Holocaust did not exist. Only rumour and idle chat by defeated minorities. No country was going to challenge the German Empire. That's what it was now. An empire of untold power.

The United States, too, had developed the bomb, but Germany were ten times more powerful and they dared not provoke the beast. Neither side wanted that war and feared they could wipe each other out.

Japan, even though they had signed a mainland truce and kept Japan free of further American attacks, had lost its territories to the United States in the Pacific as Hitler—despite being an ally of Japan—had no interest in the far east and left them to their fate against the Americans. Russia had rebuilt but had no military force of note. Hitler had allowed any conquered states a small local force to help keep the peace and secure its borders. Germany ruled Russia and bled it for its vast resources, just as when Stalin had won, and Russia spread communism across eastern Europe after the war. Russia was then the great threat to American democracy.

But now it appeared there was only one great superpower: the German Third Reich, with the Americans as a distant second to Germany.

Neither were interested in fighting a war, and nuclear weapons had changed all that. They were now at peace and had an open trade policy with each other.

Germany allowed certain countries to have democratic rule, but ultimately, they all answered to one power.

No country was allowed a significant military force, and everyone fought on behalf of Germany.

Except that there were no more wars to fight. Was that the last great consolation? There were no wars of note. Israel did not exist. The Jews were indeed wiped out in Europe, and there was therefore no one to settle in the Middle East. From 1943 to 1965, Germany ruled these regions with an iron fist and therefore there were no uprisings, no oil to fight over. In his last two years alive, Hitler had allowed some countries, like France, England, Ireland

and Belgium, to become democratic as, with the world becoming more technological, he wanted to ensure they could run themselves and not rely on German finance indefinitely. Upon his death there was a massive state funeral and his body lay in state in the renovated Reichstag building, massively increased in size and splendour by Hitler's Chief Architect Albert Speer, for ten days of mourning.

His successor was a man called Bernhard Ebert, a high-ranking advisor to Hitler, who the German cabinet felt could hold the reins during this time. Ebert was a non-military man, and it was thought that he would be the perfect man to bring Germany into the next century in a peaceful way.

I closed the book and put it back on the shelf and felt so saddened by what I had seen. A terrible but important part of history just wiped out. Looking around at people browse through the many books on sale, I thought *this is it. This is their reality. They know no different. It's what they have been born into. They have no idea what the real truth is. They have been schooled in a Germany history. A victor's history.* It was not their fault. I knew that.

It was my fault. It was Hoitdle's fault too: he had lied to me. But I was drawn in, seduced by my own selfish curiosity, a curiosity that had gone too far. I bowed my head and walked out of the bookstore. As I stepped back onto the street, I looked up at the clear sky and knew I had only one course of action left in my being. And I would do everything in my power at the very least to fix that.

And so, I set off towards home to plan my next and final move. I had to go back and find Hoitdle.

Heading down Henry Street, I found myself looking at people's faces. I don't know what I was looking for, but they didn't look the same. They had a strange kind of emptiness. They seemed different. Not as jovial as I had always known Irish people to be. They seemed—dare I say it?—German-like. Could we have changed that much from German influence over sixty years? I glanced once more at a swastika flag hanging outside an old store-front blustering in the warm breeze and once again felt a deep shame as I now hurried my steps towards Connolly train station, where I could catch one of the many buses that went by it in the direction of Marino and home.

As I arrived at the opposite side of the station it was strange to see the many flags of Europe alongside the swastika at the centre. I guess it was normal to everyone else, who now had grown up in a world of a Nazi-ruled Europe, but to me it was incredibly odd. I had to get home. I had to see if my family were still the same.

What if I had changed so much that they didn't even live there? What if I had no friends? Would Paul even know me? I had to assume that as I was still alive, that my parents had existed in the present. I knew my dad was gone, but I wanted to see my mam and my sister, Shelly. Perhaps if I had changed their past to the extent I had done with Germany and the rest of the world, then they wouldn't have conceived me. Who knew? My mind was racing with so many thoughts now, that I almost missed the next bus. I got on, paid my fare with some coins I found in my pocket and sat down in an empty seat at the back of the bus and looked out the window as it pulled away. I took in my new surroundings as the bus made its way through the traffic. Most of the buildings I knew were pretty much the same. I guess the only thing that had changed in this new world was me: I was the stranger in their world now. Here in Ireland, I was walking amongst a generation of Irish Europeans of such German influence that only I would be the one who would know what we used to be.

Fifteen minutes later I saw my stop approaching. I headed to the front of the bus, ringing the bell along the way and waited. The bus pulled into the stop and I stepped off and waited for the bus to pull away. When it had, I looked around and remembered the last time I was here. I looked across at Fairview Park and watched people jogging, pushing buggies and playing with their kids. It all seemed so normal. I started to walk and there I passed by O'Connor's café where I had met Hoitdle to discuss the start of our devious plans. I stopped and stared in at the very table where we had sat, and I had a vision of us talking there. I closed my eyes and wished myself to get up, walk out and never see him again. Alas, it was too late for that now. I walked again and got to the edge of the road to cross the street towards my apartment. I could see the door and wondered if it was still mine. Crossing the street, I remembered Sara and thought how I would have loved to bring her home with me. To meet my family, friends and to show her my Dublin. I got to the gate and went through. I headed up the steps and stopped at the door. The moment of truth: I had always hidden a spare key under a rock near the side wall of the front garden. But this time, I could not see the familiar rock. I walked over to the area and scouted around to see if maybe it had been moved, and just then the front door opened.

"Can I help you?"

I was startled and turned to look up at who had spoken from my door.

"Oh hello, my name is John. I was looking for someone who maybe still lives here?" I said, thinking on my feet as I hadn't prepared for the possibility that this could have happened.

"Who are you looking for?" The slim lady was looking at me suspiciously. She was about forty years old, sounded Polish, dyed-blonde hair and wore tatty jeans and white shirt. Her shoes where white flats with no socks and she had a worn face. I walked slowly towards her trying to look over her shoulder to see inside. I could see my home was no longer mine. The paint colour was now light blue and peeling and my dresser was gone. She asked again "Who are you looking for?"

"Oh, I'm sorry – I may have the wrong house, but do you know a John Ryan?" I asked her.

She looked me up and down and replied while shaking her head. "No, I don't know him, I'm sorry," and she went back inside and started to close the door.

I rushed to it and said, "Wait, sorry, can I ask you one more thing?"

She was taken aback and said, "Please sir, I don't know anyone by that name. Now let me close my door, or I'll call the police."

"Please, just let me ask you one more thing and I'll go. Please, miss," I pleaded. "Have you lived here long?"

She paused for a bit, looking at me, and then replied. "I've lived here for only two years with my husband, but my parents have been here before me for nearly thirty years."

"Thirty years," I said out loud.

"Now go, I have to go," she said and as I took my foot away from the door, she closed it hard and I heard it lock from inside. I stepped back and I looked up at the windows and then turned and walked down the steps slowly and out the gate. Taking a last look up at the place I used to call home, I now knew some things had changed and I would have to try figure out what else had changed. How was I going to fit back in here I thought to myself? Where would I go now? Would my mother, my sister and Paul still know me? Surely, they were wondering where the hell I've been for all this time. How would I explain it? In the new world, what was I? Who was I? Was I still a college graduate? The history I was studying before I left for Germany was certainly a changed history now. So, what was the new John Ryan doing?

For all I knew I could be a truck driver in their world or a fast food restaurant worker.

I had to head to my family home to find out. It wasn't far from where I was and could walk there in under fifteen minutes. And so I headed off towards Griffith Downs, just off Griffith Avenue.

Arriving outside the house, I felt apprehensive about going in, after what I had just experienced back in Marino in my old apartment. But I had to know. One way of the other, I had to see what my new life was going to be. My family home was a four-bedroom, redbrick, square-shaped house, with a small front garden just off the main road, and had vines running down the front walls. The red door I had always known was still the same. I just hoped the people living behind it were still there and intact. I approached the door and could hear voices inside. I paused for a second and took a deep breath. I knocked three times on the door using the large brass knocker and waited. I heard someone come to the door and it started to open. I can't tell you the relief when my mother opened the door and smiled right at me.

"Hello son," she said.

"Hi Mam," I replied, and I fell into her arms to give her a big hug.

With a chuckle, she asked, "Is everything alright? We've been worried about you."

"I'm fine, Mam, just happy to see you, that's all," I replied.

"Come in, I have the kettle on, I'm making tea for everyone," she said. "Your dad and sister are out in the conservatory, go say hello and I'll bring it out with some nice homemade cheesecake." She smiled, knowing it was my favourite.

I was taken aback by her comment. "Mam, what do you mean, Dad is here?" I asked, wondering if she had lost her marbles.

"Yeah, he's in the conservatory talking to your professor friend. Oh, and ask him if he takes milk in his tea, John," she asked.

"My friend," I replied inquisitively. "Is Paul here?"

Then my heart dropped as she said, "Paul who?" I had known Paul for five years now, and my family had known him all that time. Something had changed and they now did not know him.

"I told you about Paul, didn't I, Mam?" I asked her.

"Maybe you did, John. I don't recall you ever mentioning a Paul before, but who knows, you can be elusive sometimes," she said. "Now go, they're expecting you." Could my dad really be alive, and here – had I changed his fate? I walked out of the kitchen and around to the conservatory. As I approached the room, I could see my sister Shelly smiling in my direction. I also thought to myself,

How did my family know I was coming and who is this friend with them? And there he was – my father, sitting in his old armchair and chatting to another person I could not yet see.

"Dad," I shouted.

He looked up and just said, "Hey, John, nice of you to finally join us."

"Hello, stranger," my sister said in a sarcastic way.

I couldn't believe my eyes. He was alive. Something good had come of this nightmare at last. As I was about to rush over into his arms, the other person in the opposite chair facing my Dad, sat up and turned his head in my direction.

"Hello, John," said the all-too-familiar voice. The nightmare was back.

Doctor Hoitdle had a wry grin on his face as he sat forward and stared right at me. "Well, don't be rude, John, say hello," my father piped up.

"What are you doing here?" I asked Hoitdle.

My father jumped in. "Now, John, that's no way to treat your guest." He continued, "Doctor Hoitdle has been filling us in on your work together. I must say I didn't realise how important it was, the work you've been doing in college, but we're all very proud of you, Son."

Just then my mother came in with the teas and cake.

"Yes, we are all very proud of John at the university, too," Hoitdle added.

"And what work is that?" I asked looking at Hoitdle.

"Come now, don't be so modest, John. Our work for the joint committees of the Irish-Germany pact to enhance our two cultures," he said. He made his intentions in being there quite clear. "But so much of what we are working on, we cannot talk about, Mr. and Mrs. Ryan. Top secret stuff, that we are unable to divulge at this time, I'm sure you can appreciate."

"Oh, of course, Doctor Hoitdle," my Mom replied, sounding so proud that her son was working on a government secret project.

And then Hoitdle said it. "We could tell you, but then we'd have to kill you all, wouldn't we, John?" He said this while staring at me for a few moments, and then in turn gave my parents and sister a look, and finally back to me. I knew what he was saying. My parents, not really getting the meaning, just laughed at his joke and my sister just smiled and rolled her eyes. But I knew. This was a threat to my family. *Keep my mouth shut or else.* Sure, even if I wanted to tell them, what could I say? No one would believe my story anyway.

Hoitdle picked up his cup of tea and smiled and just continued talking to my father about old times like they were old friends. I was numb and asked myself if this was all some weird dream that I was unable to awake from. But no, it wasn't. It was real. A living nightmare. As I listened to my family hang on Hoitdle's every word, I wished I could talk to someone about this. I wished I could talk to Sara. The only other person in the world that would understand. I wanted to throw my arms around my dad, but he would think it strange, as to him and my family, everything was as it should be.

"Well, I could sit here and talk all night, but I must leave for the city. I have an important meeting and, well, they are real slave-drivers and I can't be late," Hoitdle said and stood up.

"Thank you, Doctor Hoitdle, for coming here today to explain where John has been, and for looking after him and giving him the chance to work on such important projects," my Dad said.

"It is my pleasure; John is very important to us too," Hoitdle said looking at me.

We all stood up and my parents and sister said their goodbyes.

"I'll show Doctor Hoitdle to the door, Mam," I said. I grabbed the doctor hard by the arm and led him to the door. I opened it and pushed him outside and pulled the door over. I led him out the gate onto the street. "What the hell do you think you are doing and how the hell did you get here first, you monster?"

"Calm down John, we don't want your family to hear the truth, now, do we?" Hoitdle said grinning. "We spent the last week repairing BETI after you ran out on us. The time you took to get home, we were able to get her working again and, well, here I am. Transported myself to Dublin four hours before your arrival. I knew you'd try to track down your old haunts. Your apartment, your friend Paul who, incidentally, won't know you from Adam. He is still alive but runs in different circles in this world and never met you. You'll find your family are really the only people who know you now, so maybe my best advice to you, John, is to toe the line, so to speak. Be a good little boy, go back inside and never speak of this again. Your time with us is over. We have achieved what we wanted, and more, and now you must live your life as you find it," Hoitdle said.

"How is my father alive?" I asked.

"Ah, you see, you have me to thank for that. Your father died of a brain seizure back in 2001, as of course you know. And why? Because no one detected a bleed on his brain during a routine check-up for a blood clot on his left arm. We used BETI. I like you, Mr. Ryan. I wanted to give you something to come home to. We went back to the night before your father was to be discharged from hospital and made the doctors scan for the bleed. They found it, and were able to intervene. They saved his life. Well, I should say *I* saved his life. And now you have your family back together, I suggest you cherish it and move on with this life you now have." Hoitdle finally finished his speech.

I didn't speak for a few moments and took it all in.

"And what now for you, Doctor Hoitdle, is that it?" I asked.

"Yes, pretty much that is it. I go home, back to Germany. Back to live my life under Nazi rule where I am a prominent man. A man of value and worth. Back to my wife Gretta, who I never told you about. She's really amazing, you'd like her. I want to live out the remaining days of my life in peace with her."

"Sounds wonderful for you, Doctor Hoitdle, but what about all the people you have destroyed along the way?" I asked.

He yelled back, "To hell with them, Ryan. To hell with the lot of them. I'm here. We're here. The Third Reich is here. Sixty years into a thousand-year Reich, we are here. Nothing else matters. This is it. This is life now. Get used to it."

I just looked at him and felt lost. I had nothing to say. What could I say? He was right.

"Goodbye, Doctor Hoitdle," I said and turned and headed towards the door of my house. My new home. The doctor started to walk away too. I went inside and as I started to close the door, I held it open for a moment just to watch Hoitdle walk away. He put on a white trilby hat with blue trim, and with his ragged old briefcase in one hand, he slowly moved along by the trees of the avenue. His shoulders were hanging down as if lamenting there was nothing left to do now, and his body seemed aged.

As he moved to the edge of the road a car pulled up and he got in the back and he closed the door. I could just make out the thick skull of the driver. It was Leitman, his trusted protector. Neither looked out at me. The car drove away, and I watched it move out of sight down the avenue, I closed the door.

Chapter 18
Small Victories

Two years had passed since that evening I said goodbye to Doctor Hoitdle. It had been a strange time of discovery. It was a new world of Nazi-led German influence and it was all the world knew. It had transpired just the way I had predicted in my paper, back in college in my old time. I had just started to blend into my new life. I had not heard of Doctor Hoitdle or any of his henchmen in all this time. I had accepted my new life.

I had gone back to university to finish my studies, but it was not the same. My relationship with Professor Hartley was different too. My dad was back in my life and I looked at the Professor differently now. That saddened me, as back in my innocent days he had reached out to me because I had had no father, and now I did. I felt I had lost a father all over again. I had made a few new friends, but it was not the same as Paul. I missed his ways. I had seen him a few times on campus, but he did not know me. He may have known of me, and said hello, but that was all. This was my new life and I had graduated and moved onto full-time employment in Dublin's Museum of Modern Histories. It was all I knew, and I worked hard to do it well, but my heart was just not in it, the way it used to be.

I often walked around the city and tried to imagine the way things used to be. It was similar but not the same and I found myself a bit of a loner and never allowed anyone to get close to me as it seemed pointless. I was afraid to get hurt again, but mostly afraid I would hurt someone else. It felt like I was walking among grey shadows of the people that went before.

It was for those very reasons I found myself back in Germany two years later.

It had taken me the last four months to find him. It had been a long journey from where I started to where I was now standing: number 16, Stenberg Street, in the leafy suburbs of southern Berlin. Two swastika flags flew high and proud on each side of the large concrete pillars that held the metal gates with an eagle adorned on them. The guard that had stood outside the front gates lay just inside the other side of the gates where I had battered him on the head with a baton.

I pulled his unconscious body behind a large oak tree and left him there tied up in his underwear. He was alive but knocked out cold. I was wearing his uniform and cap and had in my hand his Glock 19, 9mm pistol fully loaded with fifteen rounds.

I stood close to the guard's hut and waited for fifteen minutes. As a blacked-out windowed Mercedes car approached, I saw it flash and I opened the gates immediately. I had watched this ritual for the past three days and waited until tonight to make my move.

I waved the lone driver through and kept my head hidden beneath my cap as the car drove up the driveway which bent off to the right and up to a large detached ground level house. There was a double garage to the right off the house which was closed at this time.

Trees lined the driveway as far as the pavement opened up and out towards the house where cars could park. The front gardens were around two acres in size and the grass was manicured to German perfection.

There were rose bushes and varied flower plots all over the garden and they were structured beautifully. A lot of care was put into the grounds.

The lone driver of the vehicle stopped the car in front of the house.

It was night-time. My watch read ten thirty, and there was some ground mist that had started to meander its way through the grounds. I closed the metal gates behind me and started to make my way up the gravelled driveway. The driver opened his door and got out. He closed his door, then proceeded to open the rear door and reached in and pulled out a brown bag that looked like groceries.

I got closer and could see the outline of the man I had learned to hate. It was Hoitdle alright. He pressed a button on his keychain and one of the garage doors to the right started to open. As he waited, he heard my footsteps and turned around, looking surprised to see his uniformed guard approach.

"What are you doing, get back to your post?" Hoitdle shouted orders. I ignored him and kept moving forward. "Do you hear me? Get back to your post, I told you! Can't you follow simple orders?"

"I guess I can't, Doctor Hoitdle," I finally replied as I now came to within about ten feet of him and looked up from my cap.

He paused and with a limp smile said, "Mr. Ryan. I suppose this day was always inevitable."

"Good to see you too Doctor Hoitdle. Or should I say, Martin Gieger?"

"Ha, so you found out my new identity, and here I am. Well done, Ryan, well done indeed," he replied.

"It took me nearly a year and a half to find you, but I knew you would turn up eventually. I knew you would be schmoozing at places where all the big wigs of the SS would be," I told him. "It was only a matter of time before you'd turn up at one of them and then I saw you. The National Concert Hall in Berlin. A tribute in song and dance to the Third Reich, playing for all Berlin's royalty and you in the middle of it. I waited patiently in the pouring rain that night until it was over and drenched in the stench of Nazi rain, followed you in a taxi to your home and watched you. I returned day and night and watched you come and go. Just enough time to see how your useless guard operated. And yes, here I am, finally. To see your day of reckoning come to pass."

"So, my dear John, what now? Are you going to shoot me in cold blood? You're not a murderer," Hoitdle said, almost pleading.

"Well, I had a very good teacher, didn't I?" I retorted.

The garage door was open fully now, and Hoitdle turned his head to look around as if looking for something or someone to help him.

"Nowhere to run, Doctor Hoitdle," I said.

"Okay, John, you win, but killing me won't change anything. I destroyed BETI. You can't go back. Why not just go home to your family and live in peace with what life you have now?" he said.

"What life?" I shouted back at him. "You destroyed the life I had. You ruined my old life and the life of many others and now I am going to end yours." As I spoke, I lifted the gun and pointed it at his head, all the while the shopping bag still in his right arm. He lifted his left hand up in protest, and said, "What about my wife? Please, Mr. Ryan, she will be devastated. Please, I am all she has."

"She'll get over it," I said with little sympathy.

As I started to pinch the trigger, I said, "This is for Sara, for Eddie, for my friend Paul, for my grandad, and for all humanity, you piece of worthless, Nazi shit."

"Sara is alive," Hoitdle shouted suddenly.

"What did you say?" I asked.

"She is alive. Leitman never killed her. He tried. But she got away," he said.

"But I heard the shot," I replied.

"Yes, you heard a shot, but you didn't see her die, did you? She fought her way free of Leitman. She ran and he missed. She got away and she's alive and well. Living a good life in Florence. Single, I believe," he said, trying to buy time with my affection for her.

"Why should I believe you? Why should I believe anything that comes out of your lying mouth?" I retorted.

"I have nothing left, do I, John? At this point in my life, I have no reason to lie now. She was no threat to us. No one would believe her story anyway, so we left her alone. She assumed you too were dead and moved on with her life. But you can find her. Live a happy life." He went on. "There is one more thing you need to know, my good Ryan. I am not the instigator behind all this. There was, and still is, someone behind me pulling all the strings. Behind us all. A higher power that we all answered to from the very start. Someone that stayed in the shadows but dangled us all like puppets. It was he who told me to find you. If you kill me, you will never know the full truth. I can help you find him and then he will answer all of your questions," Hoitdle said in a hopeful voice.

"I'm done talking. And I'm done with all your deceit and lies. I just don't care anymore. I don't give a damn if there is some mystery puppeteer still out there in the darkness. Let him stay there. Let him rot in hell for all I care, if he even really exists. Maybe he's you. Maybe he's in your head. Either way, I'm still going to kill you Doctor Hoitdle. You know that to be certain now, don't you?" I said with ease.

Looking forlorn, beaten and out of words, he nodded his head and raised his free hand high to the sky and began to shout. "*Heil,*" was all he managed to yell as he fell to the ground with a single gunshot wound to the head and he collapsed in front of me, letting the shopping spill out all over his driveway. It was my last piece of defiance to him and his Nazi party to deny him the chance to scream out *Heil Hitler.*

The blood spilled from his head and out onto the ground as I watched it seep through the gravelly stones, and I turned and walked away. A few moments later I heard the screams of an old lady. It was his wife Gretta who came out to find the remains of a man who she knew as her king.

She fell to her knees beside him as she tried to shake him awake, "Martin, Martin," she yelled. "Please, wake up, no, Martin, no." She lifted his head onto her lap and tried to grasp at any sign of life. There was none. It was too late. She screamed out for help as I let her cries fade away behind me as I kept on walking.

She slowly got to her feet with her clothes drenched in the treacherous warm blood of her dead husband.

Her teary eyes looked down the misty driveway to see who could have taken her world away. All she saw was the empty driveway and the open metal gates with the Swastika flags lying somewhat still now. That's all she saw. The empty street of where a man once stood. A man whose next destination was Italy.

The End.